D1285674

THE QUEEN
OF DIRT ISLAND

Also by Donal Ryan

The Spinning Heart
The Thing About December
All We Shall Know
From a Low and Quiet Sea
Strange Flowers
A Slanting of the Sun: Stories

THE QUEEN
OF DIRT ISLAND

Donal Ryan

VIKING

VIKING
An imprint of Penguin Random House LLC
penguinrandomhouse.com

First published in hardcover in Great Britain by Doubleday, an imprint of
Transworld, a division of Penguin Random House Ltd., London, in 2022

First American edition published by Viking, 2023

Grateful acknowledgment is made for permission to reprint the following:

Extract on p. vii from "History" from *Gaudent Angeli* by Mary O'Malley is
reproduced by kind permission of Carcanet Press, Manchester, UK.

Extract on p. 66 from *The Flowers of Evil* by Charles Baudelaire, translated by
James McGowan, is reproduced by permission of Oxford Publishing Limited.

ISBN 9780593652930 (hardcover)
ISBN 9780593652947 (ebook)

Printed in the United States of America
1st Printing

Set in Adobe Garamond Pro

This is a work of fiction. Apart from the historical figures, any resemblance
between fictional characters created by the author and actual persons,
living or dead, is purely coincidental.

To my mother, with love

Let the books remember the local battles.
Re-write the plot. Let the harvest wither.
This is your life. She is your great event.
Keep her in the sun.

'History', Mary O'Malley

END

S he was born.
    Small but healthy, a fortnight early. Through a soft misty rain on her third morning her father drove her home, slowly, swaddled tight against her mother's chest, her mother kissing her cheek over and over.

Her father's face was rough and tired from work and lack of sleep. He couldn't stay to see them get settled because he had to go straight to work, so he left his wife and his first child alone in their newbuilt bungalow in a small estate at the foot of the hill where he'd been raised, where all his people before him had farmed the land and lived their lives.

His heart was light as he drove away. He was doing his duty by his woman and this new woman who was his daughter, these two people he was sworn to provide for and protect. The obligation was heavy but would be worn lightly. He'd never shirk nor resent the burden of this work he had now to do. Everything had a glow about it, a sharp halo of pure light, and the long straight road between the village and the town stretched itself before his car obediently. The sun had pushed itself up across the new day, the rain had stopped and the clouds were washed and bright.

A figure in the distance, hunched and dark-suited, slouching towards the town, turned half around at the sound of his engine, and stood to wait. He slowed and stopped and reached across to open the passenger door from the inside and the man sat in, a man he knew, a man whose sons were his friends, whose daughter he'd courted for a while one long summer years ago, a man he liked and respected and who smelt on this spring morning like yesterday's drink, a smell safe and familiar, like apples windfallen and turning rotten.

God bless you, the man said. Any stir? And he smiled and told the man his news, and the man slapped his own knee and offered his bony hand across to shake the new father's hand, saying, Well now, well now, God is good, welcome to her, welcome to her, and may God be good to her all her days. What'll ye call her? I don't know yet. We don't know yet. Eileen wants to wait a little while. To see what name reveals itself, she says. And the passenger laughed then, high and loud, and slapped his knee again. That's a good one! Ha-ha thee, faith, I have it all heard now. Reveal itself! Well, anyway, it's as good a way as any. What's in a name? A rose by any other name would smell as sweet.

And they were laughing as the creamery truck rounded the only bend between the town and the village of the new father's ancestors, and thundered towards them wide of the centreline, a good shade too fast, and in a flash and a heartbeat both men ceased to be.

BLOSSOMS

She was four in her earliest memory, or maybe just turned five.

It was springtime so it must have been near her birthday. The cherry blossom tree was heavily flowered at the edge of the small front garden; it was itself the greater part of the memory. Or maybe it was her birthday, because someone was taking a photograph and she was standing beneath the cherry blossom tree with sunlight dancing green and pink across the grass, her grandmother on one side of her and her mother on the other side, each of them holding one of her hands, as though they might at any moment start to tug in their opposite directions and pull her clean apart.

But that violence must have attached itself to the memory afterwards. She surely hadn't thought it at the time. What was clearest about the memory was their reflection in the long window at the front of the small house, how clear it was, the tartan of her mother's short skirt, the heavy grey of her grandmother's cardigan, the way they were linked to each other like a daisy chain. And the back of the man who was taking the photograph, long and white-shirted, his head bowed downwards to the old-fashioned camera that he had held out from himself, low down below his stomach.

Why did she remember the image of his back so clearly

and not his front, his face? Why had she fixated on their reflection and not their realness? It never happened anyway, her mother told her years later, when she asked who the man was that had taken the photo. I can guarantee you, she said, that no man stood out there on that lawn and took a photograph of you and your grandmother and me. Where is it, so, if it really happened? The photograph. Did you ever see this famous photograph at your grandmother's house or here in this house or anywhere else for that matter?

She wondered why her mother was so adamant about the memory's falseness. She knew her mother was wrong, of course. It had really happened, almost exactly as she said, with just a few details up for argument, like whether or not it had been her birthday, and who the man was that her mother said never existed. It could have been one of her father's brothers, though neither of them had long backs, or some relative or other who had faded from their lives. It could have been a neighbour. It could, she supposed, have been a boyfriend of her mother's, though her mother denied that she'd ever entertained a suitor, even for a moment. Her husband might have been gone from this world but he was and always would be her husband and that was all there was to it now for good and for glory. The memory was real, though. The cherry blossom blazing pink, the grass warm under her feet, her grandmother's hand, her mother's soft hand.

FREEDOM

Saoirse was the name that revealed itself.

Freedom. Once in the kitchen she heard her mother saying maybe it was foolish. A foolish choice. I wasn't in my right mind and Father Ambrose even asked me at the time was I sure and of course I said I was. He asked would I not consider Mary, after you, or Bridget, after my own mother. Maybe I should have, Mary, should I? If she ever goes to America the Yanks won't have a clue how to pronounce it.

But Nana retorted, Yerra Yanks my eye, what in the name of God and His Blessed Mother would cause you to worry about some Yank getting his tongue in a knot in some far distant time? What do you or any of us care about that shower? We owe the Yanks nothing, girl, least of all the consideration of pronounceable names. All they ever did was twist names to their own ease, anyway. That place is full of O'Brains and Mahonerys and Mulligrews and Contertys and names that never existed because the donkeys on Ellis Island couldn't be bothered their lazy arses to write down people's names properly that were falling starving off of the boats and nor could their descendants that got all the jobs in the offices giving out visas and such.

Nana went on and on for a while like that, and she started to pretend to be one of the people in the office in America where people went to have their names made shite of, talking in a loud put-on accent, and her mother was laughing so much she could hardly take a pull of her cigarette properly. Anyway, said Nana, when the laughing was over. We had no choice but to call her that good name. After all the battles our people fought along the years against the English to be free. There were martyrs made on every road of this country. And Saoirse pictured Nana on her daily walk the two miles down from the farm on the hillside above the village, praying for the dead that lined the road.

She saw then from where she was sitting at her jigsaw on the floor in the doorway between the kitchen and the sitting room, almost out of the sight of her mother and grandmother, that the two women were holding hands across the table, and they were looking down at their joined hands. She wished in that moment that she could join their sadness, for the man in the photos over the fireplace and along both sides of the hallway with the dark hair and blue eyes and shining smile, father to her, son and husband to the women in the kitchen, but she couldn't. She felt about him only a deep curiosity, about how he had ever existed above his grave and outside of his own photographs, how she was exactly half of him and half of her mother. It was all a wonder.

FATHERS

Every other house in the small estate that had children in it also had a father, a living one.

None of them looked like they were of much use except for cutting grass with the same shared lawnmower, taking turns to cut the verges and the small green area at the front of the estate and the smaller green at the back. Most of them worked in the town four miles from the village, leaving in the mornings wearing jackets and coming home in shirtsleeves, smoking as they parked their cars. Some of them drove vans with their names on the sides or the names of businesses, advertising their services, a plumber, a carpenter, a wholesale butcher, an electrician.

The butcher had a smiling cow on the side of his van. The cow had long eyelashes and bright green eyes. Nana thought it was very funny that the cow looked so happy. Look at her off, God help us, as happy as the day is long, not knowing she's for the high road. The poor old cows have an awful life, you know. Pregnant nearly as long as they're alive, never by choice, and their children whipped from them one after the other.

One of the fathers cycled to work and his children would wait at the front of the estate for him every evening. Saoirse would watch them from the front window, sitting on the wide sill, leaning her forehead against the cool glass. They'd start to get excited when they heard the sawing creaking noise of his bicycle chain on its cogs, the smaller one, the boy, hopping from one foot to the other and pointing out to the main road at the junction near the estate's entrance.

When their father rounded the corner at the junction and was in their sights they'd run towards him shouting, Daddy! Daddy! Daddy! at the tops of their voices, reedy and shrill, and she would sometimes hear her grandmother say to her mother, Will you listen to those children, the screeching out of them. What in the hell has them so excited? The same commotion every single day. I'd say they're a bit touched. Eileen, are those two children of the Joneses imbeciles or what are they? They couldn't be the full shilling anyway. Running out onto the main road like two leverets. You'd think the mother or the father would have them warned against doing that. Lord. Some people haven't a dust.

Living fathers, then, weren't much of a thing. Better to have a mother who smoked and wore sunglasses even when it wasn't sunny and had long hair, not like the other mothers whose hair was mostly short like their husbands', and a grandmother who was your mother's mother-in-law who walked down to see you nearly every day, and a father who was dead, forever young, sitting on a chair at a table with his own father and all his dead relations, playing cards, waiting for Judgement Day.

POISON

It came in a letter.

One sunny day as she was lying on her stomach on the grass in the back garden, watching a beetle's black and purple back as it climbed a furry stalk towards the flat green leaves of a strawberry plant, Mother shouted from the kitchen, BASTARD! The sound of it travelled through the small house and out of the back door to the little garden, over the scraggly thorny bushes and the butterflies, the potato patch gone wild with weeds, the dandelions that turned from yellow umbrellas into fairies made of cottony light and flew away with one breath. All across that tangled city, that world of humming peace where a million tiny creatures lived their lives, all of which she loved, even the wasps, Mother's shout rolled and broke like a thunderclap and even the grass seemed to shiver in fright.

She rose to her feet and moved along the garden and the gable wall to the open kitchen door where she stood. Mother's and Nana's heads were nearly touching across the table, and smoke from cigarettes and steam from cups of tea ascended towards the ceiling in wispy, twisting clouds. One of Mother's hands was holding out a sheet of paper and the other hand was over her eyes and Nana was reaching for the letter. She raised her chin to read it through the bottom part of her glasses. Her head moved from side to side. As Saoirse crept closer to the door she could hear, softer now, almost in a whisper, her mother saying, Poison. Jesus Christ almighty, isn't that pure poison? How could he do this to me? My own brother. And I adored him, you know, I adored him. I'd have died and gone to Hell for him. How could my family believe such evil things?

And Saoirse heard her mother's voice breaking, cracking into pieces that came out of her in a line of ohs, oh, oh, oh. And Nana then, shushing her. Shush now, girl. Don't let the child hear you. Here, look, there's only one place for this kind of a thing. And Nana rising then and moving from her view towards the side of the kitchen, and the sound of the stove door being opened, and then slammed closed again. Now. That's the end of that foulness. Don't even think about it ever again. Anyone that blackens another like that will have to account for their words before Our Lord. And how will they explain themselves? Lies are the devil's language, and greed is grist for his mill.

Best to crawl back to the garden. To blow the dandelion fairies into the blue sky. To leave to the big people all the words so poisonous that they needed to be burnt in the stove. Slut, whore, bastard. They were all just sounds. And Mother and Nana, if you only waited, would always start to laugh again, and the world would find again its perfect peace.

MYSTERIES

They'd always surface again, though, those mysteries. Eavesdropping was a way to solve them, but it demanded patience. Clues were elusive. She tried to remember a time when her mother had sat with her and told her anything of any substance about her own life, about the life she must have had before she met Saoirse's father, about her childhood or her teenage years or early adulthood. Had she had many boyfriends? Had she ever been anywhere? England or Europe or even Dublin or Cork? Saoirse knew she'd gone to a private school in Limerick. Something Hill. A picture always occurred to Saoirse when she imagined her mother's schooldays, of her mother walking along an avenue of yellow flowering bushes in a pleated striped skirt and white-edged blazer and prim knee-high socks, a straw boater cocked sideways on her head, but she knew that she was superimposing images from her Malory Towers books and the girls of Saint Clare's on her ideas of Mother's girlhood.

She realized that she and her mother rarely spoke properly at all. That most of Mother's speech was indirect, utterances flung around like fistfuls of confetti, vaguely aimed and scattered randomly. But she supposed this to be the way of all parent and child relationships. Her mother told her every single night that she loved her. I love you, my doty, as she tucked her

II

in. I love you, my little sweetheart. My jewel. My perfect girl. And when she was too old to be tucked in Mother would say the words as Saoirse went to her bedroom, drawing her towards her if she were sitting down, sometimes fully into her lap, even later when she was grown to nearly her mother's height, Goodnight, doty, goodnight, my sweet love. That was surely enough.

Mother had Nana to speak to about the important and boring things that occupied older people's minds. They sat at the kitchen table and whispered at each other, and sometimes she would still herself and train her ears to the rhythms of their voices, picking out random words from the smoky air. Things about Paudie and Chris and what would become of them, and how they'd never manage to divide a living between them from the bit of a farm, and what would happen if one of them wed, or both of them, but there was little prospect of that anyway, thanks be to God, for the time being. About someone called Richard, and Mother would say the words Daddy, and Mammy, and Aunty Elizabeth, and ranks of grim-faced, dark-clothed phantoms would array themselves before Saoirse's inner eye, and string themselves out along the cold stony shore of Mother's past, her secret other life, their mouths downturned in disapproval. And Saoirse was content to wonder and speculate and to draw inside herself vistas of possibilities, to build a castle of towers and battlements and to let it fill with all of Mother's whispered ghosts, all the sorrowful mysteries of the world.

BLACKBIRD

Something banged one summer evening against the glass of the front window.

Mother and Nana started up from their seats and hurried outside, Nana blessing herself as she went. Saoirse followed after them, scared and curious. At the front of the house Mother and Nana stood looking around but there was nothing, and no sign of anyone out on the road or in next door's garden or along the hill or over on the green. That was only someone blackguarding, Eileen, Nana said, young fellas probably, firing stones. But Mother didn't answer, she was standing at the window looking down at the line of flowers where the narrow walkway beneath the window met the lawn. Among a cluster of grinning pansies, its little neck bent and one tiny glass eye still reflecting the light of the sun, lay a blackbird, not much more than a hatchling. Oh, Mother was saying, oh, little darling, you silly little thing. Nana looked and rolled her eyes and dismissed the dead bird with a wave of her hand. At least it wasn't bowsies anyway, she said. I'd hate to think that there were bowsies pelting stones around the place.

Nana went back inside but Mother didn't move. He never got to live his life, the poor little love. Saoirse tried to speak but she wasn't able to make any sound: a painful lump had formed itself in her throat, like she'd swallowed a stone. Tears were falling from her eyes and pooling at her chin and dripping from there onto the front of her dress, and she could hear someone making a low moaning sound. She looked around to see who it was before she realized it was herself. Mother had knelt down and picked the dead bird up in her hands and she was lifting it towards her face as if to kiss it, when Nana reappeared at the corner of the house and said, Eileen! Don't put that maggoty fecking thing near your mouth! God only knows what it was carrying!

But Mother pretended not to hear her, and she kissed the blackbird on its lifeless wing before laying it back on its peaty deathbed. Saoirse turned and ran for the road, Nana shouting after her, Where are you going? And she shouted back as she ran, The priest's house, so he can do the last rites! and she could hear Nana shouting, Don't you dream of going near Father Cotter and he not a wet week in the parish, he'll think we're all away with the fairies, looking for sacraments for birds!

But the priest didn't mind. He crossed the lake road back to the estate, holding Saoirse's hand in his, and Nana met them halfway down the avenue, apologizing for her granddaughter's terrible imposition, and he said it was none at all, and he whispered a prayer above the blackbird, and Mother dug down into the flowerbed with her trowel, and they laid the baby blackbird in the earth.

ARMAGEDDON

What would the end of the world sound like?

Like someone chewing with their mouth open. Chris or Paudie or even Mother, as dainty as she'd act. When Saoirse went through the village and across the main road and up the hill to Nana's farm, she'd try her best to get out of eating there. Her uncles always arched themselves across their plates, elbows out as if to protect themselves and their food each from the other. Will ye go handy, Nana would shout, go handy let ye in God's name, and don't choke. Then she'd stand behind them and fondle the backs of their heads and look from one to the other with a kind of a foolish expression on her face.

Saoirse would eat her food quickly too, watching across the table for the specks that flew from her uncles' mouths when they spoke, and now and then a speck would make it all the way across, and she wouldn't be able to finish whatever concoction she'd been given. Nana wasn't a good cook. Signs on, Mother said, she's down here most evenings for her dinner and a pot of God-knows-what left simmering above for the two boys. Mother would say mean things about Nana sometimes but if an evening came that Nana was expected and didn't arrive she'd stand at the window watching for her, wondering out loud where she might be, asking Saints Anthony and Christopher to keep an eye on her, or Saint Jude if it got very late. The silly cow could get killed crossing that road, the speed the cars go through the village. Something needed to be done.

The real end of the world would be Nuclear War. Mother had a book about it that had been delivered the same year that Saoirse had been born. Mother read it sometimes, smoking fags and saying, Sweet Jesus. Nana said, If you saw the yahoos that gave out those books, Scaldy Collins and a few more dipsticks, going around tormenting people. The book said that everyone should practise getting under the table if it came on the news that a nuclear bomb had gone off, and putting a blanket over the table and weighing it down. The world would be filled with *fallout* but you'd be grand if you stayed under the table.

Mother said one day, We should practise doing it. The nuclear drill. But Nana grabbed the book out of her hand and threw it into the stove. Now, she said, watching the stove suspiciously for fear, it seemed, that the book of terror might somehow escape the inferno. Let that be a finish to that foolishness. You may as well worry about the sun forgetting to rise in the morning. All that talk is made up to keep people fearful and to give idle men an excuse to be swaggering around giving orders, telling people to obey them or die. A gobshite's charter, it was, fit for nothing but flames.

ANNIVERSARY

Our departed brothers and sisters.

How strange that sounded to her, having neither. And her father's name then in the list, every year, two days after her birthday, or sometimes three. She'd always feel Mother and Nana shift slightly in their seats when his name was read out, and Nana would sniff or make a tiny sound in her throat, like a whimper, only barely hearable, and Saoirse knew that she only heard it because she was listening out for it.

They'd walk the road then to the graveyard, except if it was raining, when Chris would drive them, and the adults would talk all the way down about the rain, where it was after coming from, how long it was going to be down for, how it hadn't been promised in the forecast. There was a path in the grass that wound from the puddled earth around the graveyard gates all the way down to the V of a stone wall in the back corner where her father waited above the fires of Hell and below the light of Heaven, under the long branches of a yew tree that Nana said was two thousand years old. Older than Christ Himself. And it'll be still there, still alive, when we're all dust. Saoirse wondered why the yew tree, with its poison berries and mean-looking leaves, should be so loved by God that it would be given eternal life.

In her ninth year she was standing in the swaying shadow

of that tree, tired from the walk and the early rise for mass, listening to her grandmother breathe her prayers into the still morning air, her eyes fixed on the green-black mould that was creeping up the base of the gravestone and along the blank space that would someday have Nana's name on it, and Mother's, and maybe her own, when she heard behind her the sound of footsteps on the damp grass. She turned and saw a woman there, and the woman was pretty like Mother but not as tall, and she was wearing a black coat and black gloves, and she was smiling, and saying, Hello, Eileen. Hello, Mary. Boys. And this must be Saoirse.

Mother seemed surprised to see the woman, happy, then sad. Sally, she said, oh, Sally. The woman bent herself a little and she put a gloved hand on each of Saoirse's shoulders, and she looked into her eyes and Saoirse could see tiny flakes of gold in the woman's eyes. Aren't you pretty, she said. Little love, you are. Our daddies went to Heaven on the same day. Did you know that? And something in the woman's voice, the sadness in the way she said the word – *daddies* – made Saoirse cry, and she was shocked at her tears, their suddenness, the heat of them on her face, and the woman took her fully in her arms then and she pressed her lips softly against Saoirse's wet cheek, whispering, Little pet. God help us.

BROTHERS

Out of the blue one day, Nana started to talk about Uncles Paudie and Chris, and about Saoirse's father.

Mercy from the Lord it was I had the three of them close together and that they were all boys. But the brains of the outfit was gone once your poor father passed away, Lord have mercy on his blameless soul. I was never able to have any more after Chris, you know. Whatever he was at inside in me he made a pure hames of my pipework. He started as he meant to go on, anyway, and that's for sure. Your mother is right about him, but I wouldn't give it to her to say it about him myself, and nor will you tell her I said it now like a good girl. But the poor boy hasn't hands to wipe his arse. And what is there for him besides farming? He'll do the basic jobs always, I suppose, the foddering and milking and the cutting of silage and hay, and anything that requires more attention and judgement can be left to Paudie. Not that he's the fucking brains of Ireland, either, mind you. They'll be a pair of bachelor farmers all their lives unless Fortune changes her aspect and smiles upon them. But there's no sign yet of her having any benevolence towards them, God help us.

Anyway, that's the sorry end of the whole thing, the way your poor father was whipped from us and they were left without guidance or any kind of a firm and shaping hand. They have hardly a memory between them of my husband, though Chris says he remembers walking holding hands with his father through the haggard and across the top acre behind the Jackman house and over as far as the Gladneys' orchard to pick apples off of trees, and being lifted up to pick the high ones that were fattened from the sun on the tops of the branches. I don't know in God's name. What must I have done to have those two fine men taken from me? At least I'd lived long enough to have transgressed. Your sins must have been done in another life.

Saoirse couldn't quite follow her grandmother's words. They felt like a stream of sparkling water that the sun was shining on so fiercely that you couldn't quite see the stream itself but just the light off it, blazing up from the earth and into your eyes, like the stream that ran down from the hills and through the village and into the callaghs where it met the lake. A stream of sadness, she thought, and she was happy with the words, thinking that she should write them down somewhere.

The poor misfortunes, Nana was saying. Alone on this earth they'll be once I'm gone. Won't you always think of them, Saoirse? The two lonesome and innocent lambs. Two promises you must make. You'll visit my grave and you'll love your poor uncles.

PASSION

Paudie was arrested.

Saoirse wasn't sure what it meant until Nana told her. Her grandmother was crying and moaning so much that it was hard for a while to make out what she was saying. Imagine. Imagine. Lord God, how stupid is he? Getting mixed up with that crowd! What am I going to do, Eileen? But Saoirse could see from her eyes and the set of her mouth that Mother didn't know what to say to Nana, what she could do to help. They both sat smoking their cigarettes at the kitchen table, and Saoirse took her customary post in the island of sunlight that formed itself in the middle of every day between the front window and the kitchen door.

Someone had asked Paudie to hide guns in the shed, down behind a load of bales of hay. And other stuff, too. Nana wasn't sure what. Semtex, Eileen. What in the name of God and His Blessed Mother is Semtex? It doesn't sound like anything that could ever do any good. And apparently we could all have been blown to Kingdom Come over it. Jim Gildea told me. You're lucky, Mary, he said. Someone was watching over ye the way it was all brought out in the open now, before Paudie was in too deep. In too deep, Jim Gildea said! As if a shed full of guns and *Sem*-fucking-*tex* isn't deep enough!

Paudie was kept inside in the prison in Limerick city for

nearly a month, and then he was allowed home. But he was probably going to have to go back to jail again. Saoirse and Mother walked up the boreen to see him. He was sitting at the great oak table in Nana's cave of a kitchen, under the brown hanging clock that Saoirse thought of as the clock of God, because there was a picture of God above it, with His two palms showing, and the wounds of the Roman nails at their centres. Paudie's hands were wounded, too, bandaged tightly so his fingers and thumbs were a fuse of gauze, and he held them out before him. I told them nothing, Eileen. The Tans. I told them fucking nothing. They done that to my fingers with a hammer and I told them nothing. His eyes were full of tears.

From where she'd been sitting in the bay window that looked out onto the muddy farmyard and the haggard beyond, Nana lifted herself, and she crossed the long kitchen in a bounding step, and she drew her hand back and struck her oldest surviving child so hard across the side of his head that he fell sideways off his chair and onto the ground and he lay there in silence while his mother raged, The Tans, the Tans, a lot you'd fucking know about the Tans, you fucking yahoo, you gom for Scaldy fucking Collins. And she raged and raged while Paudie lay supine, holding his wounded hands up towards the risen Christ.

PROPOSAL

Chris proposed to Mother.

On an evening in early summer with his working clothes on him, as though he'd been seized suddenly by some amorous impulse, some wild desire that had been lying dormant, he came rushing down from the fields to the village. Half cocked as Nana said later, though she didn't wholly disapprove of his hastily conceived and poorly executed plan. He stood a long while at the side door mumbling. Saoirse had never seen a redder face. Mother had stepped back to let him in. She had a cigarette just lit and she was pulling on it deeply. Come in, Chris, she said, through a cloud of blue smoke. I won't, Eileen. My boots are covered in muck. I won't drag it in along your clean floor. Clean, my arse, said Mother, and Chris laughed, a high chuckle, the way he always did. Chris enjoyed Mother, and she liked him right back.

From somewhere, from the ether or the blue heavens or the fumes of new growth or agricultural diesel, he drew courage, and he made his proposal. Eileen, I was wondering, Saoirse heard him say. Wondering what, Chris? I was wondering if it wouldn't be the best thing, for all concerned, if you and me, if I and you, if you and I . . . And then he said it straight, nearly in a shout, Will you marry me? Saoirse saw Mother bend forward as though someone had struck her in the stomach, and she grabbed in her two fists the lapels of Chris's overalls, and pulled him into the kitchen, slamming the door closed in the same movement. Chris's eyes were opened wide in shock. Whatever he'd been expecting, it wasn't to be manhandled off his feet. He straightened himself and put a hand over his face and drew it downwards, as if to reset himself, to regain something of his passive countenance.

What kind of rubbish are you talking, Chris? He didn't know, it seemed, what kind of rubbish he'd been talking. But on he ploughed. We wouldn't have to, you know yourself, be married in the fullness of the word. We'd just, you know yourself, take the bad look off of things. You'd have, you know, a bit of company. Yourself and the baby. Baby? Saoirse was eleven years old, and she opened her mouth to protest this slight, but some vague wisdom rose from within her and silenced her. Paudie and Chris called her the baby, and maybe they always would.

I love you dearly, Chris, said Mother. And I'd be a lucky, lucky woman if I was free to marry you. But I'm still in my heart and soul married to your brother and I will be I'd say for all of eternity.

Chris said it was okay. He was sorry. And Mother said she was sorry too, and she kissed his cheek. And Chris dragged himself back up the hillside and he didn't come down again for a long, long time.

HANDLEBARS

Heavy the blooms, Eileen.

Wasn't that the first line of a song? Mother didn't know but Nana went away singing it anyway, making up her own words. On her way to the main road she passed a boy on a bicycle, no hands on the handlebars, a hurley tucked under his oxter. You'll break your neck, young Gleeson, doing that, but the boy just laughed and said, Hello, Missus Aylward, and cycled on, shifting his weight to the left to turn in to the estate, and to the right to turn in to the short driveway where Saoirse and her mother stood. The way he steered the bicycle with no hands looked like something as magical as the trapeze people at the circus in Nenagh might have done, something impossible, right in front of you.

Hello, Eileen. Hello, Saoirse. She wondered how he knew her name. He was wearing shorts and a hurling jersey in the parish colours. He had red cheeks and blue eyes and his arms and legs were the longest arms and legs Saoirse had ever seen, longer even than Paudie's or Chris's, and there were green grass stains on his legs and his shorts. He ought to cycle away home and have a bath for himself, Saoirse thought, and her thoughts were in Nana's voice, as they often were. It was funny to think of what Nana might say in any given situation, to think in Nana's voice.

Mother was looking at the boy on the bicycle in a cross way, and when she spoke to him her voice was whispery, and she looked sideways at Saoirse before and after she spoke. Go on now, Jamie, go home and clean the grass off of yourself. That struck Saoirse as fantastically funny, how Mother had said the thing that she knew Nana would say, or a version of it, and she laughed out loud.

Will you come to my twenty-first, Eileen, please? the boy said. Or maybe he was a man. There was some hair above his lips and white shiny hairs on his arms and legs but he hadn't the grizzly rough look of older men who had skin like pork chops. I will not, Mother said back, in her sharp that's-all-there's-to-it voice. I'd look well. You would, Eileen, you always look well. And Mother turned towards Saoirse and said, Lovey, will you please go into my bedroom and get my handbag off the bed? Good girl. But she stood just inside the side door, and she could hear Mother saying, You know you can't just arrive here like this. The neighbours will be fattening on the sight of you. And then the boy-man was saying, Eileen, please, and Saoirse on a sudden impulse blocked her ears, and when she looked out again the boy was cycling down the avenue towards the lake road, his hands on the handlebars now, and Mother was standing in a patch of white sun, looking up at the sky.

STORIES

Have you any news?

Stories were everywhere. You could listen or you could choose not to, but the stories would find their way to all ears eventually, and you could believe them or you could choose not to. Stories came in from Nenagh and down from Portroe and up from the lake and down from the mountains. Nana called in on her way home from devotions many a Sunday evening bursting with news. Saoirse had never been to devotions because Mother said it was just extra mass and once a week was more than enough for anyone. One Sunday evening in particular Nana came in full to bursting, a smell from her of incense and sweat, a fevered aura about her. Before she even had her gloves or hat taken off, before she laid her missal down, from just inside the door she started to speak, and her voice was shrill with excitement.

Mother seemed to sense that Nana's news was unfit for Saoirse's twelve-year-old ears because she told her to go on outside and Nana stopped and pursed her lips but she was moving up and down like she needed to pee, and Saoirse lingered near the slightly opened sash of the living-room window to see how much of Nana's story she could catch, but she couldn't make out the names, just the fact that the story was about a pair of dykes. Saoirse didn't know what that word meant but Mother's voice sounded cross when she repeated it. Dykes! Where did you hear that disgusting word? Nana said she'd heard it plenty of times. You'd be surprised, lady, at the words I hear. Anyway, it's true. They were seen holding hands and canoodling down the callaghs several times by several reliable witnesses. What do you think about that?

I don't think about it, Mary, Mother replied. They're fine women and what they do together is their private business. Private business? They have a right to keep it private, then, besides broadcasting it to all the living and the dead. Fine women, how are you. What do they even do to one another, I don't know. It doesn't bear thinking about. Mother shouted then, suddenly, so loud that Saoirse felt her eardrums vibrating. DON'T FUCKING THINK ABOUT IT, THEN! JUST SHUT UP, SHUT UP, WILL YOU? Mother and Nana were silent for a good while, on into the darkness, Mother going about her tasks with a censorious air, a simmering brusqueness, and finally Nana rose to go. She'd been waiting stubbornly for a softening, for an apologetic approach, for an opportunity to regain Mother's good graces. I'll be off, then, she said from the door, and she knotted her headscarf tight below her chin. A full minute passed or maybe more, and Mother said, Oh, fuck it, anyway. And she hurried into the moonlight to make up with her mother-in-law, her dearest friend, to see her across the main road as far as the end of the boreen.

GIRLS

There were lots of stories about girls, how girls used to be. There was the girl who used to wait out at the yellow bridge for truck drivers, the lads who did the long hauls, and she'd do things with them in the layby out at Derryhasna. For money or because she wanted to, nobody knew. She never had the look of a one that had any bit of money. And who knew what impulses overtook people? Nana didn't know, anyway, and nor did Mother, and if they didn't know then Saoirse hadn't much hope of knowing. But what was it to know a person, anyway? What could be known about them except the outside of them, their eyes and nose and mouth and the sounds that came out of them, the particular way they had of moving through the air?

There was the girl who worked inside in the saucepan factory that had affairs with several of the bosses and ended up nearly running the place until she had a slipup and had to go off to England to get sorted out and when she came back her clocking card was gone from above the clock and her pink slip was folded into the slot where the clocking card used to be. No apology or explanation was offered and nor did she go looking for one, as smart as she thought she was. She'd had her day in the sun and it was a long day but the night drew in again the way it always does.

There was the girl who walked along with her widowed father and her brothers silently and always behind them or to the one side of them in a frock that looked like it was bought in another time and patched to death and back to life again, with rims of dirt about her neck and her ankles. Her lip was often split. Her eyes were often black and blue. She wore these injuries apologetically, as though she knew the discomfort they caused people to see them, how conjectures weighed on them, how their prurience discomfited them; she made people mad with guilt for the pleasure they felt at her punishments.

There were the girls who tried their damnedest to be good and good they were. Good girls who gave their parents pride in the way they conducted themselves. Who got married to the men that asked them and were grateful, and didn't go looking across the brow of their hills to the hills beyond to see to know how much greener was the grass, who bore children who were good and quiet at mass and sat still and said their prayers to God.

Ha, said Nana. We all knew those girls. Didn't we, Eileen? Did we fuck, said Mother, and they laughed, those lovely women, they laughed. Oh, but look. What could be known about people in their privacies? No eyes could see beyond a closed door or into a heart.

BOYS

There were boys, too, of course, just as many.

There was the boy inside in town who went up to the Christian Brothers as happy as the day was long with all his pals, swinging his bag along the road like boys do, climbing trees for the first of the conkers and firing them around the way boys always have and always will as long as horse chestnuts grow and flower. And one day he accidentally fired one at the car of a teacher, a long fellow with a wicked temper, and the teacher said nothing but parked his car and went into the school and when the school day was well under way he went into the classroom where the boy was sweating the day away waiting for the comeback to happen, hoping against hope that it was being forgotten about. And all his hope was dashed when the long fellow stood at the door and said, I want to borrow one of your fine boys a minute, and the girl who was teaching the conker-thrower's class had nothing to say except, Go on, go on with Mister Clanchaert now, and Mister Clanchaert threw the boy against wall and floor and kicked him in the stomach, and the boy from that day on had no regard for anyone that claimed to have authority over him; nor was he ever carefree again.

There was the boy who played hurling like hurling was never played before, hardly touching the grass as he ran, twisting his body around like a thing not even human, bamboozling his opponents with his skill. And the day after a county final where he scored in every second minute of the match and was carried off the field in glory he went into his father's hayshed with a rope and strung himself up. How had he no mercy for himself? Not seventeen years alive and nothing he could find in the universe to live for, to live out his three score and ten and whatever extra bit he might have been given. Or a greater part of it than he allowed himself. What in the hell could have been so bad? Lord, have mercy on the boy.

There was the boy who drove the van and delivered firing for Joss McGrath, who was always covered head to toe in black dust, and it was comical to see him coming in the driveway and only the whites of his eyes and his two front teeth glowing out from the blackness of his form, and he always, always smiling.

There was the boy who left his daughter and his wife one morning early, and his daughter not halfway through her first week of life, and drove away to do his day's work, as happy as a man could be, as good a man as man could be, and met his death on the bend of the road near Nenagh.

God help us, God help us, God help us.

YARNS

There were happy stories, too; Nana's yarns.

Sometimes Saoirse thought about them in bed, imagined herself writing them down, so that everyone could read about the impossibly ancient world of Nana's girlhood. But maybe the stories wouldn't be as good without Nana's voice. Like the one about the chickens and her first holy communion cardigan. Her dress was borrowed from her cousin Dymphna, who'd made her communion a year earlier, but Dymphna wouldn't part with her lace cardigan, even for the day. Nana's father and her brothers were gone to the bog, so her mother said, Come on, we'll take six chickens into Nenagh and we'll sell them to Danny Costello and we'll get you a cardigan in Hodgins's with the money. Daddy nor no one will ever know.

We made a busht down the boreen so fast to catch the midday bus, said Nana, we nearly met ourselves coming back. Lugging a canvas sack of chickens each. But the bus was late, of course, like always. My mother stepped out onto the main road to look in towards Limerick to see could she spot it and didn't a big huge car stop to see were we in need of help. The man driving it was very grand so Mammy suddenly was very grand, too. My *hosband* is cutting *torf*, says she, otherwise he'd have driven us in his *mowtor cawr*.

We got into the car anyway and I got car sick like I always

did. Around Riggs-Millers, I opened my sack and puked in on top of the chickens, and the chickens of course popped out, and went berserk around your man's car, and shat all over his leather seats, and by the time we got to Nenagh you could hardly see the poor man for the cloud of feathers inside in his lovely car and the clumps of puke and chicken-shit. But he said to Mammy, Don't worry, I'll get a valet. I took off crying then because I thought he said to Mammy, I'll get your wallet. Mammy explained to me what a valet was and I cheered up considerably, and Danny Costello handed us over a ten-bob note and a good fist of coins for our chickens, and he passed no remark on the terrible condition of one of the sacks, and we got my cardigan in Hodgins's and we had tea and scones in Quigley's café with the change, and we bussed it back home and had the churns washed and the cows in and the supper made before the boys arrived back up from the bog. And no one ever knew, nor did anyone ask, how my cardigan was paid for bar me and Mammy. Daddy kept no account of cardigans or chickens. Isn't that a great story?

Mother sometimes rolled her eyes and shook her head at the outbreak of a yarn. But she'd always listen all the same, and smile at the end. And that was all that Nana ever wanted.

WORK

Something had run out.

Saoirse couldn't make out exactly what was being said, but she'd been told to stay outside; the door was closed, and the kitchen was full of smoke and urgent whispers. Nana was saying, There's no need, Eileen, I have plenty, and Mother was saying, No, Mary, no, Mary, I have to. Saoirse went to stand at the big tree near the entrance where the estate children congregated. There was a boy there from down the lake road who was a year older than her, or so she presumed, because he was a year ahead of her in school. She couldn't stop looking at him, the way his eyes shone and the way his hair fell sideways across his forehead. He didn't seem to see her so she pushed past the Joneses and the Walshes and prim little Loretta Cleary in her white dress and frilly socks, and before she knew she was going to do it she pushed the bright-eyed boy as hard as she could and he fell backwards onto his arse.

He looked up at her in wonder from the ground, and laughed, a kind of breathy laugh. The group of estate kids who'd been in his thrall stared at her wide-eyed. What's your problem? he asked, drawing his knees into his chest and folding his arms across them as much as to say he'd been planning on sitting down anyway and it was all the one to him. She badly wanted to say something funny, something smart and devastating, something that would make him feel small and ignored, the way she'd felt as she'd been looking at his eyes and his hair and the rips in the knees of his jeans while he'd been looking everywhere but at her. Something she'd heard Mother say about the man who gave out books from the mobile library drew itself to the front of her mind, and she heard herself say to the fallen boy, You're some fucking poncey-looking prick.

The boy roared with laughter then, and he hopped back up, brushing himself off and fixing his fringe. Saoirse felt someone jostle her lightly in the back. Oonagh Jones, she guessed, who'd always had a bit of a thing about her, who never chased her when they played Bulldog from the top of the hill to the end of the avenue, and acted like she didn't exist.

I'd better say nothing back to you, the boy said, or Paudie Aylward will come down from the mountain and blow my kneecaps off. Or is he already in prison? Fuck off, Saoirse shouted, and turned for home. She heard him saying behind her, I was only joking, hey, Saoirse, I was only joking, and the sound of her name from his mouth thrilled her, though she wasn't sure why.

The smoke had dissipated and the door was open. Nana and Mother were sitting in silence, drinking tea. The argument had ended itself. Mother was going to work.

BOOKMAKERS

I t turned out well.

Mother started work at ten so she was able to get the half-nine bus in the mornings and she finished at two so she was home before Saoirse finished school, and there was no difference high up or low down, really, except that Mother wore makeup every day and spent a long time looking at herself in the sitting-room mirror in the mornings while Saoirse was having her breakfast.

The job was in a bookie's. Bookie was short for bookmaker. Saoirse imagined Mother placing pages carefully in their proper order and gluing the ends of them into their covers, while other people drew the pictures that went onto the covers and the people that wrote the books stood waiting with their stories piled high up in their arms. She knew, though, really, that Mother didn't make books. The bookmaker had something to do with horseracing, and, from what Saoirse had seen of it on television, horseracing was the most boring thing on earth. She wondered why the world tried to make itself so mysterious, why things were given such misleading names.

Mother worked on Saturdays, too. One Saturday she and Nana waited in Quigley's bakery for Mother to finish. The café was closing at five and so was the bookie's. A few minutes before five, Nana said, Run next door like a good girl and have a peep in. There was no window on the wall or door of the bookie's, just a high opaque pane that stretched across its width, and a metal sign bolted where the window would be with a picture of a horse leaping a fence and a jockey in white and green leaning forward onto the horse's neck.

As Saoirse opened the door she saw her mother behind a high counter at the shop's far end, and a small group of men huddled before it looking up at her. A bald man was sitting beside Mother behind the counter, hunched over, counting something, it looked like, because his hands and mouth were moving in unison. One of the men in the bunch was raising himself up towards Mother and he was holding a piece of paper in his hand, and he shouted something that made all the other men laugh. Mother reached out with her left hand and took the piece of paper from the man, and at the same time swung her right hand around in a wide arc and slapped the man into the side of his face. The bald counting man looked over and shook his head and turned back to his counting. Mother examined the piece of paper while the slapped man stood back from the counter holding his hand to his face. The men around him roared and shook with laughter. Good girl, Eileen, one of them shouted. And facing his chastised comrade he said, Jesus Christ, Frank. Surely you know better than to give that kind of lip to a one from Dirt Island?

VISITATION

An old black car rolled into the driveway one Sunday afternoon.

Mother looked out the sitting-room window and staggered backwards, saying, Oh, no, sweet Jesus, no, sweet Jesus, no, no, no. Saoirse had been lying on the couch in her mass clothes, wondering dully about who might be out on the road, whether it was worth going outside, whether she should change her clothes in case there was a game starting on the green. She still had homework to do. Secondary-school homework took over the whole weekend, between the awful dread of it and the doing of it. Mother's histrionics roused her but only a little. Who is it?

Mother didn't answer, but she shrieked suddenly, Get down to your room, right now, down to your fucking room, and put on a long skirt or jeans or something, just cover your fucking legs, go on, NOW! Mother was suddenly beside her, dragging her by the arm, then pushing her through the door into the kitchen and across the kitchen towards the bedrooms. Three knocks, firm and loud, echoed through the house. Mother sobbed. Oh, Jesus, she said in a whisper, and Saoirse saw tears in her eyes. Mam, what the fuck is going on? But Mother didn't answer, just said, Shut up, shut up, put on a long skirt, and don't stir from that room until you're called.

A large man dressed all in black like a priest but for a white shirt beneath a strained waistcoat and a heavy overcoat though the day was mild, and a woman tall and thin like a reed, dressed darkly, too, stood in the kitchen. Saoirse could hear their voices, low and insistent, their words being formed slowly, and long pauses between each utterance. Mother's voice was low, too, monotonous, tapering, sapped, it seemed, of its energy. From the shadows of the hallway through the cracked-open door, Saoirse watched as the man took off the hat he'd been wearing and she heard Mother clearly now because her voice was higher, and she was half laughing as she said, Daddy, you're gone as bald as an egg!

The reedy woman spoke then, in a sharp voice, refined like Sister Michael but shriller, Why wouldn't he be as bald as an egg as you say, and the poor man pulling his hair out over you all these years, and he hardly able to sleep at night? Thinking of you in this – this place, and he never once having laid eyes on his grandchild. Mother shouted then, SAOIRSE! COME HERE! And she went out and hauled her daughter from her room and into the kitchen and stood behind her with her hands still tight on her upper arms, and the two strange people regarded her silently, the big man with a look of benevolent amazement on his face and the narrow woman with a haughty, pursed expression, and Mother was shaking her a little now, saying, Look. Take a good look at my beautiful child.

KNOWLEDGE

All the things about the world that can't be known.

What happens inside people's hearts. Why people fall in love with each other and fall out with each other. Mother said she loved Saoirse's father from the second she saw him. That couldn't be true, but Mother insisted. She insisted too that there was no man like him in the world, none as good or as brave or as handsome. Saoirse had studied the photos around the fireplace with greater concentration and intent as she got older, to see could she find in his eyes and in the lines of his nose and mouth and chin what Mother and Nana said was there, to see if she could draw from his images some of his greatness, or awaken in herself some quality that must be latent in her, dormant, waiting to be stirred and used so that she could be adored the way it seemed her father was.

She wondered at her own lack of wonder. About the enormous things that must exist behind her mother's eyes and in her mother's past. Why had Saoirse never wondered why she'd never met these people before? She'd left her mother's childhood and girlhood and womanhood in a small bowed box in her imagination, pristine and untouched; there was after all no mystery about it, just that there'd been a falling-out, and there was no need for any expansion on that stark term, falling-out. Mother had come one day to the town of Nenagh and she and

Saoirse's father had chanced upon one another on Barrack Street, and he had bid her good day and she had bade him good day back, and this small exchange had parlayed itself into a conversation, and into a courtship, and into a marriage, and into a child being born, and into God reaching down His omnipotent hand from Heaven and directing a swift and violent end for the good and handsome man, He Himself only knowing why, and no good could ever come from questioning His divine authority, but hold on.

Hold on a second. Here was a date at the bottom of the picture, written in white letters and numbers slanting forward. It had always been there, she knew the date by heart, but it had never occurred to her that the date was the date of her parents' wedding, October first, 1982, exactly four months and twenty-two days before the day she was born, and now here she was a teenager and only now was it all coming together in her head. Why there'd been such a falling-out. Why she'd never seen these people before. They were ashamed of her mother, and ashamed of her. And her dead father and her dear Nana and her uncles, one a jailbird and the other a simpleton, and they had come in their old, posh-looking car, it seemed, to remind Mother of their shame, and Mother cried for the rest of the day once they'd left.

PROTECTION

A red-faced lady called one evening in early autumn as the sky yellowed in the west.

The lady was small and round, with short curly hair. She was buttoned tightly into her coat, and seemed out of breath. Mother bade her sit down at the kitchen table, and the lady hefted a brown briefcase onto the table and opened it with two loud clacks.

Nana was standing by the stove and Mother was drawing a chair back to sit down and saying, What's this about now, Concepta? You might as well tell me straight out, and Nana suddenly blessed herself, a sure sign that there was some threat, some danger afoot, perceived at least. This is Saoirse, is it? the lady asked, and nodded towards her. You know well it is, Mother replied brusquely. Who else would it be? The woman reddened more deeply, and said, She's small for her age, isn't she? Is she twelve? She's fourteen, Mother said, and you know that well too, Concepta Quirke, haven't you a file inside in your briefcase with every detail of my child's existence written on it? Come on now, lady, out with it.

Concepta Quirke? Nana suddenly said. Are you Nonie Quirke's daughter? I am, the lady said. And what are you doing going around to people's houses tormenting them? Are you not married? I am married, the red-faced lady said. I've been married five years now. And would you not go home and look after your husband besides driving the roads looking for trouble where none exists? It's my job, the lady said, and Saoirse's curiosity now was at a screaming pitch inside her; she wanted badly to know who the lady was and what torments she was inflicting on people. She found herself enjoying Nana's interrogations and the way that Mother was smiling at the woman, dragging on her cigarette and blowing the smoke in a thin line over the lady's head; she could feel the disdain that Mother felt for the dumpy short-haired woman, her easy superiority.

Go on, Mother said. Tell me, Concepta, what's on your mind? What kind of a poison-pen letter did you get this time? Am I a prostitute or a murderer or a gunrunner or what is it now? Now, now, the lady said, there's no need to be like that. Not half there's not, Mother said. Come on, Concepta, get it over with. *Coronation Street* is starting in ten minutes.

It was about Mother's job. There was an allegation that Saoirse, a minor child, was being left alone in the house while her mother, a single parent, was working in Thornton's book-maker's in Nenagh. Mother drew a sheet of paper from her handbag. There's my roster, Concepta Quirke. I only work during school hours. And her grandmother minds her on Saturdays. I do, said Nana. Go on home now and make your husband's supper, Concepta Quirke, and ask God for His forgiveness when you kneel tonight to say your prayers.

FEAR

That wasn't the finish of it.

Mother was summoned by letter to Nenagh, to an office by the hospital, where she had to wait on her own while Saoirse was brought to a room by a lady who looked like she was at least as old as Nana. Now, lovey, she kept saying, as they walked down a corridor with long tubes on the ceiling for lights. Now, lovey, here we go.

In the room sat Concepta Quirke. In the few weeks since she'd come to the house she seemed to have gotten younger and thinner, or maybe she was just more comfortable here in her own territory, with no Nana chiding her, with no Mother blowing smoke in her face. She wasn't red and buttoned up in a heavy coat; she was wearing a white billowy blouse and she had lipstick and eyeshadow on. She smiled at Saoirse and looked at her for a long while before she spoke.

Now, Saoirse. You must tell the truth. Have you ever been left at home on your own? No. Have you ever been introduced to people in your house who made you feel uncomfortable? No. Have you ever woken up to find your mother left for work or otherwise absent from the house? No. Does your mother ever entertain guests? What does that mean?

She imagined Mother as a cabaret singer or a magician, performing for people in a spangled costume with fishnet tights and a top hat, dancing and twirling a baton and pulling rabbits from her hat, with a line of people on the couch and armchairs and dining chairs, clapping and whooping. It means, Concepta Quirke said, does your mother ever have friends over, for a drink, or for a meal maybe, or does anyone ever stay overnight in the house. No, no! Mother hates most people!

She hates most people? Ya, and she really fucking hates you! She says that my father told her you were a fat fucking goody-two-shoes in school and everyone laughed at you and you were wearing a bra when you were eight and everyone called you Bazongas Quirke. And when you left our house that time my nana and my mother laughed at you for about an hour and Nana said your husband had a gimpy leg and cod eyes and water on the brain!

Saoirse heard herself shout all these things in her head, but her mouth didn't open so the sounds never came out. She felt pain in the palms of her hands and she realized that she'd been digging her fingernails into her skin. Concepta Quirke was looking at her, and she was asking her why she was crying, but she couldn't answer, even though she knew. She was crying because, for the first time in her life, in this office of a woman whose job it was to protect children, she was afraid. Saoirse Aylward was fourteen years and nine months into her life before she felt fear.

EXPULSION

The boy she pushed was expelled from school.

What she liked most about his story was how he didn't tell it in a boastful way. He just leant back against a post of the fence between the front green and the road with the estate kids in a semicircle around him, staring at him as he spoke. Oonagh Jones poked her bony elbow into Saoirse's side as she pushed through to the front and Saoirse kicked backwards and felt the sole of her runner connect with Oonagh Jones's shinbone, and she heard a screechy, hateful noise from behind her, and Oonagh Jones whispered, You bitch, your mother is a prostitute.

His name was Oisín. What a beautiful name. It sounded like waves breaking. He was acting his story out as he told it. This teacher, it was like, our second or third time having the cunt, for French, I didn't even fucking want to do French, and he comes right down to where I was sitting, and he says, Show me your book, show me the page of the book we're on, and I had no book, my mother hadn't got it for me yet, and I said, I have no book, and he grabbed my hair, here, at the back of my neck, and he pulled up as hard as he could, and I only boxed the cunt because of the shock I got at the pain of it. Did anyone ever do that to you? And Saoirse realized then that he was talking directly to her, but Oonagh Jones answered, Ya, Sister

Benedict is *always* pulling our hair, she's a fucking wagon. But Oisín just smiled at her and looked back at Saoirse again, and said, I have to go home now, the parents are gone fucking doo-lally since I got fucked out. They brought the priest down and all to talk to me. Here, Saoirse, do you want to walk down the road with me?

Fuck's sake, said Oonagh Jones. Fuck you, Jones, said Saoirse. When I come back you're dead for calling my mother a prostitute. And she followed the boy onto the lake road and they walked down the gently sloping hill in silence, and she wondered why he'd asked her to walk with him if he wasn't even going to talk to her. What age are you? he said at last. I'm fifteen she said, adding a year to her age, and she wasn't sure why. Oh, we're the same age, then. No, actually, I'm fourteen. Why did you lie? I don't know.

He took her hand and his hand was cold, and he held it tight and didn't look at her. You're a gas yoke, Saoirse Aylward, he said, and all she could think to say back was, Thanks. They walked to the quay and sat at the water's edge, their toes touching the surface, and after a long time he kissed her softly on the cheek, and again she said, Thanks.

REPOSE

After fifteen years of life she saw her mother's home.

It was given the name Dirt Island, Mother said, because everyone was jealous of it, and couldn't bear to see my grandfather, who was a blow-in, do well out of it. It wasn't his fault he was left a farm. He'd been in England, in Liverpool, breaking his back on the docks. He brought back an English wife, my grandmother, and two small babies, twin boys. They're gone now, my uncles, God rest them. They both died young. But my grandparents had three more once they were over here. That was a small family in those times, wasn't it, Mary? And Nana agreed that, yes, it was, especially for big farmers that could afford to keep as many as they wanted. Chris spoke up from the driving seat: Childer is aisy shtock to get into. Ah, shut up, Nana said. A lot you'd know about it. Chris drove on, red-faced, silent.

The island that gave the farm and the townland its derogatory name was in the middle of a small lake downhill from the ancient three-storey house that was Mother's childhood home. The island was a hump, really, yellowish-brown in colour. Chris parked at the far end of the yard from the house and stood staring at it. Nana hissed at him to come on.

The cobbled yard and the rooms of the house were full of people who had a familiar aspect, a way of speaking and moving that Saoirse knew well, because it was Mother's way of speaking and moving. Some of them shook hands with her and said things like, Ah, now. Look who it is. The famous Saoirse. She saw her mother hug a woman who looked like she could be her twin, and an older woman watching on with her mouth downturned, who whirled about as soon as the embrace was over, as if to escape any possibility of having to interact with Mother.

Mother stood in the good room of the house she'd been reared in, and Saoirse stood beside her. The dark bald man she'd met just once before stood across from them. Between them lay his wife, reposing, her cheekbones pushing out against her white-green waxy skin, her lips a straight thin slash. Her rosary beads were light blue, twined around her fingers, and her fingers looked like they'd been glued together. Oh, Mammy, Mother was saying, over and over again. Oh, Mammy. And the bald man, Saoirse's grandfather, was saying, Now, now. She's gone to her reward. We'll see her again someday, please God. We'll see her again.

Daddy, why didn't you tell me she was dying? I didn't know, the old man said. Don't you know how she was with her secrets? Don't you know, Eileen, how stubborn she was? Stubborn, said Mother. Stubborn. Daddy, why were we all so stubborn? It's just how we are, I suppose, the old man said. God forgive us our sins, it is.

ISLAND

The day stretched on and on.

She stood in the long parlour in a semicircle of strangers. A shuffling queue of mourners filed past. Some of them stopped to ask, Who have I in it? Are you so-and-so's daughter? Some of them widened their eyes in shock at her answer, I'm Saoirse Aylward, Eileen's daughter. Nana and Chris stationed themselves in a shadowy corner of the kitchen to wait it out.

A man walked across from the far side of the dead room and said, Come on with me. She looked for Mother but she was gone. The man took Saoirse's arm gently in his hand and steered her through the front door and along a narrow causeway between two great puddles where the yard sagged. He stopped at a wall and pointed down at the lake with the island in its middle. He told her it was formed from a streak of alluvial soil which ran right through the loamy soil of the rest of the farm, and seemed to spout upwards from beneath the lake. This was Mother's brother, she suddenly knew. Richard, taker of the cherry tree photograph. Richard of the poison words.

Every summer we lived out there, me and your mother. We were king and queen of that island. We used to make rafts and we'd camp outside until all hours. Saoirse looked at the side of his face. He was very handsome. His hair was jet black, swept back from his forehead. He had a slight hook in his nose, and dark eyes, heavily lashed. Her mother's eyes. He pointed then along a grassy lane that led away from the cobbled yard. My mother and father built all those sheds and the slatted house and the milking parlour up there by hand. Literally. They dug the foundations out with shovels, and set the steel and poured concrete and laid every single block themselves. Just after they were married. My mother, God rest her, was left a strip of land alongside the lake field over there by her own father and so we expanded out that east side. And every blackguard and waster around here started to call the whole place Dirt Island, out of envy and spite. He turned back to Saoirse, and his dark eyes looked into hers. He lowered his voice to a near-whisper.

Your mother broke my parents' hearts. She's a whore. Do you know what that is? And all Saoirse could do was nod. There was nothing she could do about the pain that rose in her throat, the pounding in her head. Go in so to the kitchen and round up your granny and your imbecile of an uncle. I'll send your mother out to you. Take a good look as you're leaving because you won't see this place again. Okay?

She nodded dumbly again, and she felt, bearing down on her from above and closing in from all sides, all the meanness and sorrow of the world.

WEAKNESS

Nana had a bad turn.

At the gap in the hedge of a field she used on dry days as a shortcut she went to hop the low stile and took a weakness as she descended the far side. Kit Gladney came on her by chance, because she'd been in the meadow that morning to see to a sucky calf that wasn't attaching to its mother, and she noticed Mary Aylward sitting on the grass, conscious but insensible, with only the barest use of her limbs. Kit ran for Ellen Jackman across the field and Ellen summoned Doctor Harvey from town, and the two women managed between them to half carry and half drag Nana to Ellen's house, where they installed her in the front room to wait for the doctor.

She'd had a mini-stroke. A transient ischaemic attack, to be exact. Sitting upright in her bed in St John's Hospital in Limerick she enunciated the alien words slowly, proudly, to Mother and Saoirse and Chris and Kit Gladney, who'd felt compelled, as Nana's saviour, to attend the hospital to drop off a novena and a relic of Saint Thérèse. Saoirse didn't like the thought of Nana staying in the stifling antiseptic room with the three other patients looking like they were taking their last breaths, but Nana seemed happy with her change of scene and circumstance, and declared that she'd been treated admirably and with great tenderness by the doctors and the nurses.

Nana looked at Kit Gladney, her neighbour and old friend, recently widowed, and she stretched a hand across and left it on top of Kit's hand. Thank God for you, Kit Gladney. It was Paddy sent you into the meadow to find me, you can be sure. The good man is walking those fields yet, and he will be until you meet him in Paradise. And wait till I tell you, a doctor walked in here earlier on, the biggest, Blackest doctor I ever laid eyes on, and I could have sworn my oath it was Alexander Elmwood coming in the door to me, and he having the same soft voice, only with a strong accent, African, I suppose.

Kit Gladney smiled at the mention of her son-in-law, seven years dead, and Saoirse watched the woman's eyes, the mingling of sorrow and happiness and plain goodness in them, and Nana, though she was laid low, seemed on a kind of a high, buoyed by her sudden positioning at the centre of events, and she said to Kit, I asked him, What carried you over here, and all the poor souls beyond in your own place falling away from hunger and disease? Wouldn't it be more in your line to look after them besides troubling yourself with the likes of me?

Kit Gladney rolled her eyes and said, Mary Aylward! I hope you didn't! And Nana seemed to have regained the full of herself now, and she laughed out loud, and said, I did, I did!

BARBER

O isín's father was a barber.

He punctuated his speech with an owl-like sound, hoo, hoo-hoo. In his backstreet shop a row of old men sat happily waiting with hardly hair enough between them to justify the flamboyance of the barber's movements, the mad blur of him, the pitch of his voice as he told joke after joke, Hey, wait until I tell you about the priest, hoo, and the prostitute, hoo-hoo, and the donkey, hoo, oh, look out, hold that thought, here he's on, my rebel of a son and the beautiful Miss Aylward, hello there, hoo-hoo, love's young dream, hoo, shove up there along the bench, boys, and let the lady sit down. Where are ye off to? The library, I hope? No? The arcade? What? Hoo-hoo! Oh, lads, to be young again, expelled from school and fancy-free!

And he straightened himself then from his labours, and brushed the wrinkled neck of the man he'd just skinned to the bone of his skull while he regarded Saoirse, smiling at her, and she laughed as he started a little shuffling dance on the spot where he stood, Hoo-hoo, hoo-hoo, if only I was young again, hoo-hoo. But he couldn't, Saoirse thought, have been that old, though Oisín at seventeen was his youngest child, and he had a brother who was nearly thirty, so the barber then must have been in his fifties, and he drew from the pocket of his white coat two pound coins and flipped them one by one to his son, who caught them deftly. Go on, son, he said. Treat the lady.

Scabby bastard, Oisín said, as they walked towards the pool hall and arcade. Saoirse thought this was unfair, and she said so, and she said that he seemed like a lovely father. Does he, really? Does he? Oisín dropped her hand and stopped on the footpath just inside the archway that led to the arcade, where the sun didn't reach and the air was cool, and they were just two shadows on a narrow lane. And what would you know about fathers?

She felt again that oppressive weight, that narrowing and closing of the world into a tight smallness, a knot of meanness and unfairness. She felt her heart shift a little in her chest, its rhythm knocked offbeat by the shock of this sudden spite. He was standing close against her and he was leaning forward so that his forehead was almost touching hers. What would you know, Saoirse Aylward, about anything? And she pushed him in the chest for the second time, but this time he didn't fall and laugh: he reached across the archway and grabbed the front of her jumper, pulling it down hard so that she stumbled forward, and she pushed him again, and ran, into the sunlight and across Silver Street and down Mitchel Street to the bookie's, where she stood in a cloud of smoke and waited while her mother, her beautiful mother, shouted the odds.

MOONSHINE

Paudie was to be released.

We can never badmouth the Orange again, Nana said. They had to agree to it, too, or Paudie and the rest would have been left to rot. Imagine how it must be paining them. Wasn't it the best of Good Fridays for us? It was arranged that Chris would drive to the prison in Portlaoise, for the good look of it, in a car borrowed from Ellen Jackman. It had hardly been used since her husband Lucas's accident that had left him insensible. Chris drove it into Nana's yard the evening before he was to collect his brother. He sat in the car a long while looking at the multitude of buttons and gauges, wondering what they were all for, feeling himself important, useful, being trusted with this leathered, powerful car, and with the task of collecting his brother, who was, according to Scaldy Collins and various other campaigners, proselytizers and fanatics, a prisoner of war.

Nana said, Look at him, he's more excited about driving the blessed car than he is about his only living brother getting his freedom. I wonder should I go with him. No, no. It's right that it should be done this way. We can't all be standing looking out of our mouths at the poor boy when he's taking his first breath of air as a free man, and anyway, there might be newspaper people up there and we'd be a show opposite the whole country if they took photographs of us.

Chris left with the summer sunrise, man and car anointed heavily with water from the holy well. Mother and Saoirse were to come up to the house for eleven at the outside, so as to be present when the boys came back. But noontime came and went and there was no sign. Nana knelt and prayed. Deliver them to me, sweet Jesus, please. Saints Jude and Anthony were invoked, all the Apostles and the hosts. The day wound itself out towards evening, the lunch sandwiches hardened and curled, the good dinner meat left uncooked. Nana couldn't speak for fear. She walked laps of the yard and she crossed the haggard over and back, worrying her beads. Saoirse and Mother offered to ring the prison. NO! said Nana, and she said no more.

The moon was high and the stars were bright when at last Lucas Jackman's car appeared at the top of the boreen. The passenger seat was empty. Saoirse and Mother and Nana stood at the open front door, and Nana was moaning now, Where is he, oh, God above, where's my child? Chris alighted from the driver's seat and opened the back door to show his mother and his sister-in-law and his niece the precious cargo he'd carried safely home, his brother, stretched along the leather seat, snoring, and the fumes of hard liquor wafting up and out and over the yard and the people in it and all of the silent moonlit land.

FATES

It got into the papers all the same.

A small piece in the *Indo* about the latest raft of prisoner releases, with Paudie's name and mugshot included. Paudie looked bruised and handsome in the photo, his upper lip swept at one side into a sneer. On the school bus Breedie Flynn said, Your uncle looked amazing in the paper. She'd never spoken to Saoirse before. She'd always been part of a twosome with Melody Keogh and they'd seemed oblivious to the world outside themselves. The lads on the bus and downtown at lunchtime called them various names, contradictory and defamatory and scabrously filthy as only teenaged boys can be: mickey-teasers, lesbians, clit-bandits, frigid-Brigids, sluts, freaks, rides, tasty, manky, gorgeous, rank; the assignations varied depending on the hue and heat of the particular moment and the particular pair of flapping lips. But Melody had started shifting Pat Shee, one of the cool group, and had entered the rarefied world of the popular, leaving Breedie behind. She was sitting beside Saoirse on the bus now, turned half around in her seat so she could look at her fully, and she was asking, What's he like now? Did he get a tattoo in prison? Is he still in the IRA?

Saoirse shrugged and yawned and looked out the window, pretending not to be excited by this exotic girl's proximity, by her livid skin and piercing eyes. Will you come to the Friary

Castle with me on Friday night? Saoirse shrugged again. Will you ask Paudie if he wants to come? No, said Saoirse. He's nearly forty, anyway. What the fuck would he be doing in the Friary Castle with teenage girls? Jesus, I don't know, said Breedie Flynn. I'd just love to talk to him, to ask him about his struggle and, you know, stuff. There's no struggle, there's no stuff. He hid some guns in a haybale, and he got caught, and that's it.

But Breedie Flynn was undeterred by Saoirse's reductive account of Paudie's exploits, her affected nonchalance; she moved closer again to Saoirse, staring, almost touching her. She smelt of polo mints, stale sweat, lip gloss, sickly sweet deodorant. I'm going to write a book about this parish some-day, Breedie Flynn said. And your uncle Paudie is going to have a starring role. I'll put you in my book as well, and your mother. She's so beautiful. Do you know they have whole rosary meetings given over to talking about your mother?

Will you fuck off? Saoirse said. She felt inside herself a hot prickle of envy at Breedie's self-possession, at the clarity and certainty of her ambition. To be a writer. To write about *her* family! I will fuck off, Breedie said, as soon as you promise me that you'll come to the Friary Castle with me on Friday night. Saoirse sighed and rolled her eyes and said, Okay, Jesus, okay, and Breedie Flynn said, Thanks. And in that moment their fates collided and were bound together forever.

DEMESNE

The Friary Castle was so packed that the guards came and shut it down.

The band had nearly finished anyway, and the townie boys had started to throw shapes at the village boys; a bottle had been flung and a tangle of bodies was heaving and spilling around the soaked floor. Outside in the cool air Breedie took her hand and they walked through the town to the castle field. There were boys there that Breedie knew, sitting on the low wall between the church grounds and the castle demesne, passing a long, rolled cigarette between them. Breedie was wearing Dr Martens and a short, tight skirt under a billowing Nirvana T-shirt; she'd chided Saoirse for wearing jeans. One of the boys had black hair to his shoulders and was quiet while the others talked nonstop, excited at the arrival of girls, each of them vying to be the alpha, panicked at the imbalance in numbers, five boys to two girls, a slim chance of any action. Saoirse had seen this before, this lunatic dance that some boys did, this frantic peacocking. One of them started up the castle wall to the arch of the doorway and sat there looking down, swinging his legs, spitting, saying, Hey, fire me up a fag, I'm the king of this castle, but his friends ignored him. Two of them had started to wrestle each other on the wet grass while a fourth was telling Breedie how beautiful she looked, how she reminded him of Courtney Love, but Breedie wasn't impressed by this. She hated Courtney Love. She'd never deserved Kurt.

The fifth boy sat against the wall smoking the end of the joint. He offered it to Saoirse but she refused. Can I walk you home? he said then. His voice seemed a little hoarse and to have a townie drawl. It's four miles, she said. And, anyway, my uncle is collecting us at two. He nodded then and said, That gives us half an hour. Half an hour for what? To get to know each other, and he turned towards her and smiled, but there was something in his face, some excess of assuredness, some practised air, that dissipated the attraction she'd felt when first she saw him. Get to know each other, she said, in a low voice, drawing out her syllables to mimic him. That's a fairly bland euphemism. Do you use that on all the girls? He laughed then and turned away from her, and flicked the roach towards his friends, who were tiring now on the ground, one of them holding the other in a chokehold, their legs entwined, like lovers spooning. The castle climber was asking for a hand to get down.

She heard Breedie from the shadows farther along the wall say, Fuck this, get off me, you weirdo, and she emerged, smoothing her T-shirt and arranging her skirt. The boy shouted after her, You fucking prick-tease, as the girls ran, laughing, hand in hand.

DANGEROUS

I never thought you'd be this brazen, Mother said.

I blame that Breedie Flynn. She's dangerous, that one. The skirt barely hiding the cheeks of her arse, and the wickedness blazing out from her through all the spots. Signs on Melody Keogh dropped her. She needn't think now she can lead you up the garden path instead. Grand for the Flynns in their big house below by the lake to be able to sort things out if she gets into trouble. You're going to town with that one now no more. Chris said ye can barely walk when he collects ye, and ye talking all sorts of rubbish on the way home in the car. And it's not fair on poor Chris having to wait up every Friday night.

Saoirse heard herself shouting now. Chris fucking loves it. He parks up outside the chipper and has a great time for himself eating burgers and perving. Nana took exception then. Don't you blacken my Chris, lady. He's good enough to make sure you get home safe from that blasted town every weekend. He does be wall-falling with tiredness every Sunday. He fell asleep at mass last week. I had to belt him several times before he woke and he roared then when he did and made a holy show of us. Father Cotter is still looking at us. But Nana couldn't keep up her crossness. You were always a good girl, Saoirse. Wasn't she, Eileen? It's not her fault that this is the way now with young ones, the dances going on until all hours and no law inside in that town. But we can't put her in a cage. All we can do is trust her.

I don't trust her, Mary. And I definitely don't trust that Flynn one. But Saoirse by now was in loving thrall to Breedie Flynn, to her green eyes like islands in a lake of kohl, her scorching pitted skin, the fretwork of scars along the insides of her arms, her livid wounds, her bruised, beautiful heart. Breedie is my only friend, she said, while Mother lit a cigarette from the butt of another. Friend, my arse. She's only using you. She has a fool made out of you, and the whole village laughing at the pair of ye waiting out at the yellow bridge for lifts to town, like a brace of tramps.

Saoirse felt herself untethered then, floating. She tried to pull herself back, but the Rubicon lay blood-red before her; she was being drawn down the slope of its southern bank, her mouth was opening now, and she was saying, Look who's talking, look who's fucking talking. Your own brother told me you were a whore, and everyone knows Jamie Gleeson's parents had to send him off to Dublin to get him away from you. I know all about you, Mother. Then Eileen Aylward struck her daughter for the first and only time, hard across her face, her hateful, beloved face.

PANTHEON

Breedie called them the Pantheon.

The golden gods, the ones who gleamed. Bobby Mahon and his girlfriend Triona Costigan, and then the younger lads that followed Bobby around like lapdogs, Pat Shee and Seanie Shaper and Pat's girlfriend Melody Keogh and whatever poor innocent bimbos Seanie Shaper was riding or stringing along at the time, and all the rest of Bobby's followers. They were always in a tight bunch in the same corner, or spread out along the dance-floor, all doing the same kind of dance, and everyone trying their best to inveigle their graces, dancing in among them, doing that fucking moronic fingers and thumb handshake with the fellas, and a fight would always break out when one of the townie boys would get smart with one of the girls or throw a dig at one of the lads.

Breedie had been best friends since primary school with Melody Keogh and now, in their Leaving Cert year, Melody had abandoned her for the Pantheon, and Breedie, but for Saoirse, was alone, and she sat in a room of bottled candles drawing blood from herself with the blade of a Stanley knife, neat cuts along her arms and legs, and she offered the blade to Saoirse but she couldn't bring herself to pierce her skin, she couldn't bear the thought of a deliberate cut, the clean edges of her flesh opening out and meeting again like the gills of a fish, and she was shocked at the casualness of Breedie's bloodletting, the rote, unthinking way she scored herself.

Saoirse knew that Breedie Flynn didn't really mean it when she said she loved her. You're so beautiful, Saoirse, you're my best friend. She had a book of poems translated from French and she'd read them slowly, in a soft mock French accent, her scored forearms still weeping . . . *But, dear, as long as dreams of yours will not reflect the flames of Hell, as long as in a nightmare's grip, dreaming of poisons, slashing blades, in love with powder, cannon shot, dreading to answer any door, anatomizing misery, tormented by the tolling clock, you will not suffer the embrace, of irresistible disgust.* She'd stop and look across the dim light to where Saoirse would be sitting on her bedroom floor, her eyes wide and filled with tears, saying, Isn't it, isn't it, like, something that tells you every truth at once? That pulls at you? And Saoirse would nod, transfixed by the melody of the words and the dim shifting light on Breedie's face, the way the flames reflected in her tears, the knowledge that she could be anyone, that it didn't matter to Breedie who she was or what she said; Breedie when she was like this compressed herself into a black hole of suffering, and Saoirse and the Pantheon and the faithless Melody and Saoirse's dead father and Breedie's dark-eyed living father and everyone and everything else in existence swirled insensate around her event horizon, sucked of light and form.

CONCEPTION

On their last night together they split a pill.

A roadie stopped them as they left the Friary Castle. Do you girls want to meet the band? They were escorted to where the musicians had set themselves up in the small green room at the back of the stage with crates of beer and bottles of hard liquor. They were downy-faced boy-men, lounging self-consciously, pretending not to notice when the girls arrived, trying to play the part of rock stars, or what they thought the part of a rock star was. It involved spread-eagling, it seemed, and heavy-lidded insouciance, languid speech and lots of look-ing at the ceiling, pulling deeply and thoughtfully on cigarettes. There'd been something about them on stage that had made them stand out from the other bands that Saoirse had seen; it wasn't in the music exactly, though the music had been good, loud, fuzzed with feedback but propulsive and soaring in the choruses, but in the way they moved around each other, the way they delivered their notes. It was a sense of preordination, of imminent apotheosis. As adolescent and pretentious as they seemed now, on stage they'd expanded into space, they'd looked like stars.

But all their glimmer and glisten was dissipated in this dank, paint-peeled backroom, and the American twang to the singer's accent as he bade them take a seat was comical. More girls had been brought to the room and the recycled breath and hash smoke and sweaty vapours were cloying, suffocating. Saoirse's head was throbbing and her throat was sore. Someone handed her a drink but she poured it into the dirty sink and drank water instead. Breedie was sitting on the guitarist's lap and Saoirse felt a hand on hers. It was the singer, and he was drawing her through the mill of sweaty bodies, winking back at her, as though she were party to some practical joke, and outside an emergency door in the cold drizzly night he drew her into himself and kissed her on the lips, and she decided to give him some rope because his kiss was soft and tender and expert: there was no frantic gobbling or biting or mashing of lips and gums, none of the teeth-clashing terribleness of the average shift.

There was a van parked near them with the band's name on the side, a big van with windows, and an open side door. He was pointing at the door and raising his eyebrows quizzically, and they were kissing again, and he really was a good kisser, she had to give him that, and he was quite funny as far as she could make out through the ringing in her ears and the lingering buzz of the tab she'd split with Breedie, and she walked with him across the tarmac to the door of the van, and all she wanted to do was lie down, so she did, and he lay down beside her, and they slept, hand in hand.

LEAVING

Why did you leave me?

Saoirse didn't know if the question was addressed to her. Breedie was sitting on the grass beneath a tree in the cold dawn at the crossroads where people from the village went to thumb lifts home. Her arms were tight around her legs, drawing her into as small a space as possible; she was barefoot, her knees were scraped, her soles were bloody, she was rocking herself and she wouldn't stand up, she wouldn't look up. Saoirse wasn't sure if Breedie even knew that she was there.

I didn't leave you. Not on your own, anyway. I went to the van with the singer. You were shifting the guitarist. I fell asleep out there. The minute I woke up I started walking out here. Jesus, Breedie, what happened to you? There was a purple bruise like a dim rose tattoo on her cheek; there was a rime of blood on her nostrils, a blue-green shadow darkening her left eye. Where the fuck are your shoes? Breedie, what happened to you? But all she said was, Why did you leave me? Why, why, why?

I swear I didn't leave you, Breedie. She heard a car stopping by the verge, and she heard a man's voice saying, Come on, Breedie, get in, and Breedie lifted herself from the wet grass and walked from under the oak's shade into the weak sunlight, and got into the car, her father's car. His eyes were flashing with anger. He didn't offer Saoirse a lift. He didn't seem even to see her. He looked at his daughter while she looked straight ahead; his lips moved and so did hers. Saoirse thought of the Tipp-Ex graffiti that had appeared around the school the previous terms: *Breedie Flynn rides her da*. The engine idled impatiently; the man's voice was raised now but she couldn't hear what he was saying with the breeze rustling the branches of the oak and the rumbling engine; then they drove away. Saoirse felt a sickness rising in her stomach, a panicky nausea, a pulsing fullness in her sinuses and behind her eyes and, inside her, a sharp, stinging pain.

Breedie wasn't on the bus that Monday. The Christmas holidays came and went without a sign of her. As winter softened to spring, old rumours were rehashed and new ones propagated wildly. She'd been taken to Limerick to the mental hospital, or the one in Clonmel for the proper loonies; she was in rehab for drink and drugs; the rumours had all been true and she'd run off with her own father; the rumours were all bullshit and her parents were going to sue the school for allowing her to be so badly bullied.

And then one Monday morning a truth took wing and rose immaculate, swooping from the shore of the lake up to the village and the town. Breedie Flynn had set herself on fire in her parents' garden the day before and she was dead.

COMEDY

She heard the first joke in the archway of the casino lane.
From the shadow of a shop doorway she watched as a boy
from somewhere up the mountains, curly-haired and freckly,
big-tongued, bovine, his legs perpetually bent at the knee as
though the burden they bore was too great, a Metallica back-
patch sewn arseways onto his stonewashed denim jacket, held
court for a mixed group of town and country lads, saying, I
don't know, lads, I don't know in the fuck how she had *self-
esteem issues*, ha-ha, I don't know in the fuck. She knew what
was coming. He was shaping, measuring his moments, building up and up. They were waiting. He was waiting. For a
straight man, a set-up. He needed someone to say it. He was on
the edge of a comedy ravine, looking for a bridge to traverse
the gap to glory. If it didn't come his joke would tumble and
die. He was leaning back against the archway wall, dragging
imperiously on his cigarette, one biker-booted foot drawn up
behind him. The moment was slipping away from him, but it
was saved, with only seconds to spare before he lost his crowd
to the afternoon mitch in the pool hall above the casino and
the school return. Why? said a small voice. Why? *Why?* the big
boy repeated. Well, I for one . . . thought . . . she . . . was . . .
fucking . . . *smoking* . . . HOT! And they roared, a bellowing,
howling concomitance of disbelieving hilarity, their mouths

opened wide, looking from one to the other bright-eyed, and they showered the raconteur with open-palmed smacks on his arms and back and head of admiration and congratulations, and they dispersed, some towards the dark casino doorway, some towards the sunlit street back towards school, repeating the joke among themselves, practising it, working on their timings, the pitch and tone of their deliveries.

In the barber shop across the street and down another alleyway the old men sat whiskered, waiting, while Oisín's father jigged and tapped and told them jokes, none of them cruel like the one she'd just heard, she was sure. He definitely wasn't a cruel man, and she wondered why Oisín had been so suddenly horrible, from where he'd dredged the darkness in himself, why he hadn't been able to contain it. She wondered if he was in the shop with his father, listening to the act, sweeping up the clippings and the dust. She missed him, his miasma of Lynx and sweat and stolen cigarettes, his uncertain swagger, his damp hand in hers. She was a different person when he'd said what he'd said; maybe he was a different person now, too.

The next morning she placed herself behind the big comedian as they exited the bus. As he shrugged his army bag from his shoulder to his hand and lifted his foot to descend the three steps to the footpath she placed her palms on his back-patch and pushed. Oh, the sounds of his flight and of his landing.

IMMACULATE

How in the fucking fuck could you have gotten pregnant? In the name of all that's fucking holy, in the name of Christ and His Mother and all the saints, how stupid are you, you stupid, stupid, stupid fucking bitch, you'll just be another fucking drippy-looking beggarwoman now going around like a miserable streel of ignorance all over the town with someone's snotty bastard child dragging out of you, you fucking eejit, after all the warnings I gave you, Jesus Christ, what kind of a fucking, fucking eejit are you, I should have known this is how you'd end up, whoring around the fucking town with that other one, at least she has the dignity of being dead, but oh, no, my fucking fool has to be landing back here up the fucking duff with some scumbag bastard's bastard fucking child, Jesus Christ, get out of my fucking sight before I fucking stab you to death, you fucking little fool, you Christing bastarding fucking bitch, I thought you were going to be something but now you'll never be anything only dirt like the rest of the sluts inside in town smoking fags outside the dole office with their turnip-headed fucking bastard children, oh, Lord Jesus, give me the strength to not fucking kill you, I'll stab you in a minute, it's my own fault letting you off into town with a hairband around your waist and the cheeks of your stupid arse on show and every dirty hound in ten parishes sniffing you, and you don't remember ever having sex with anyone, well, isn't that a good one, that's the best I ever fucking heard, the pregnant virgin, look out there, Mary, and see can you see the three wise fucking men coming down the hill with our gold and our frankincense and our fucking myrrh, look out and see can you see the Holy Spirit and the North Star, our lady is after having an immaculate conception and she's going to give birth to the king of all men, in the name of God and all the hosts of angels what do you take us for, and my fingers worked down to the fucking bone for you since the day you were born, and your poor father below in his grave, well I'm glad he's not here to see it, the day come that you'd blacken his name and his memory, you needn't think now for a single second that I'll be raising your bastard for you now, lady, you can clear the fuck out now and get a house in town like the rest of the little bitches, I'm not looking after you now any more, you're big enough and stupid enough to land yourself in the shit now it's nothing but shit, this life, start to finish, I thought you were different, I thought you'd be something, God forgive me, it's my own fault for trusting you, I thought behind it all that you were good.

REMEMBER

It's just proving them all right.

That's the killing thing, Nana agreed. The killing thing is how all the smart ones will be fattening now, saying, For all their minding of her, ha-ha, and all their praising of her, and all the talk about how she was a great girl, they couldn't keep her from letting herself down.

Nana stayed away for a week and a day. Longer than she'd stayed away before in Saoirse's memory. Mother didn't cook or put on makeup or go to work, just sat with the curtains closed, smoking and crying, breaking now and then into a renewed tirade. Saoirse lay in bed, too tired to argue, feeling about her body a vague expansion, a sudden heaviness, as though the pregnancy was accelerating now that it was in the open, as though the baby felt free now to flourish inside her.

In the place between wakefulness and sleep, in the soft blue light through the thin bedroom curtains, in some part of her mind that worked in its own way at its own ease, dim, formless impressions hardened themselves momentarily into memories. She had to let them take their own shapes. She couldn't impose any direction on them; she had to shut off her recalcitrant will, her stubborn consciousness. Then a cold hand would point to the inside of the van, point to her lying on a narrow bunk with the singer, feeling so tired and so heavy that she could only close her eyes and sleep, she had no choice, as good a kisser as he was, as gentle the touch of his hands. The cold hand pointed to the van's side door sliding open, people looking in and laughing and shutting it again, the singer waking, his long hair tickling her cheek as he raised himself on one elbow to look down at her, Hey, hey, are you awake, and turning around to look up into his face, and his face getting closer so she could smell staleness on his breath and cigarette smoke, and his lips on hers, and his body on hers, him saying, Are you sure? and her saying, Yes, yes, and a rhythmic movement between them but only for a few moments, and her thinking that couldn't be it.

And nothing more until the dawn shone weakly through the narrow window and she woke alone, fully dressed but for her shoes, which were placed neatly side by side on a counter facing the bunk, and she stepped down from the van, her head pounding and her eyes stinging, and a feeling that the world had emptied itself of everything living but for her, no sign of the singer or of Breedie or of any of the people from the night before, no birds even in the grey-white sky, and in her ears only a distant ringing sound, her lips dry and in her mouth a bitter taste.

Maybe she was still asleep and this was all a dream.

SAINTS

Paudie and Chris came to the door.

We want to see Saoirse. Do ye now, indeed? Ye can see her all ye like once ye don't be petting her and telling her she's great. The pure solid show she's after making of me. Paudie looked cross then. Go handy, Eileen, go easy on the girl. She's not the first to get into trouble nor will she be the last. The day is gone that a girl getting pregnant is any kind of a shame. It's no one's business now, only ours, and we'll look after it. Mother stepped back from them, into the sitting room. Chris pulled the door closed and the two men stood in the front porch, unsure of what to do next. They never looked comfortable down here in the angular lowlands of the estate. They were shaped to the contours of hills and hedgerows, their feet only sure on giving ground. Saoirse wondered how Paudie had lived all that time in jail, in an unyielding world of concrete and metal. She sat with her hands across her bump, her feet up on a pouffe, in her dressing gown.

Anyway, whatever about that. Will ye try and talk sense to her about her exams? She says she won't do them. This tactic seemed preposterous to Saoirse. What would Paudie and Chris know about exams? Paudie had left school at fifteen and Chris followed suit a year later, and she didn't think either uncle had ever passed an exam. Paudie raised his chin and looked towards the ceiling, for inspiration or succour, it seemed, or to see if something might be handed to him from above, channelled through his bulky form from the ether, some universal wisdom or insight into the best course of action for a pregnant girl of seventeen to take, what could be done to ameliorate this situation for everyone.

We'll look after you, Paudie said. Mother sighed wearily. But she'd stopped looking angry for the first time in weeks, and Saoirse could see that the light through the window was glinting off her eyes, where tears were gathering. She looked tired. Paudie's face was red now and sheened with sweat. The exquisiteness of his discomfort filled the room from corner to corner, like Mother's cigarette smoke. Chris fidgeted beside him, looking wildly about, anywhere but at Saoirse and her handful of extra flesh wherein was growing a whole new human being, a new part of this strange little family, a person with a mouth that would one day speak, please God, and eyes that would one day see, and ears that would hear what goes on in the world outside its mother's skin, all the absurdities of it, the idiocy and fear and kindness of all these people and their wounded loving hearts.

And then Chris said: Remember, Eileen, how you were put to shame. We won't ever do to Saoirse what was done to you. We'll never ever make her feel ashamed.

FUTURE

Nana came around.

Whatever about the future, she said one day, worrying about the past is the hollowest of all things. She said she saw a programme one time about that scientist fella with the moustache and the funny hair, and how he declared that you could travel through time but only forward. And you had to travel nearly as fast as a ray of sunlight to break free of the clock. There's no going back for man or God or any creature that ever lived. We can only go back in our minds and even then we're going back to something that doesn't exist except the way a dream exists. So we can forget changing the past and all we can do is look after our present moment, planting good seeds in it so that our next moments might be fruitful. Isn't that right, Saoirse? Aren't I right? I am. So as cross as your mother is or was or as regretful as you might be it's all the one now for good and for glory. You're landed as you're landed and you may as well make the most of it. You'll only be judged by the holy Joes and Mary martyrs that have themselves yoked still to a notion of the world that's gone. Some people love being ruled. Signs on we let the foreigners walk all over us all these years.

Saoirse knew that there were things she could have done but it was too late now. And she knew she didn't have the courage for any of them. Or did she need more courage not to do those things? The house that felt sometimes as though it might close in around her and crush her to death was still a place where she was mostly happy. Out beyond the low rooftops and across the tops of the trees that lined the edge of the estate and the Youghal Road there formed from cloud and broken bits of blue an abstract shapeless mass of possibilities, infinite variations of herself, and none of them could be known unless she plucked one down and examined it to see what it contained. Her hands when she felt these thoughts assail her fell to her stomach and the warm place there where the baby was insisting on its own accrual into human form, and she resented it and loved it and was frightened by it, the force of the power that it already had over her, the power to make her lose herself, her sense of herself as a person who could move unhindered through time.

Mother kept humourless vigil in the evenings now, watching her, pretending not to be watching her. I suppose we'll never know the pup that did it, will we? And Saoirse told Mother, It was a singer in a band, and Mother shook her head and pursed her lips and repeated the words in a tired voice, A singer in a band. Sweet Jesus wept.

FORTUNE

Mother softened enough to tell a story.

A good story. It seemed as though the story itself had a purpose outside of its own telling, that the details of it all mattered, that the telling of it in this moment mattered. She wished she could write the story down exactly as Mother told it so that she could read it back to herself whenever she wanted.

You were sick one time as a baby. Remember that, Mary? And Nana nodded her head slowly and said, Yes, I do. Mother said she hadn't known what to do for the best. Saoirse had been feverish, hot all over and a wet shine from her skin, and she hadn't cried, that's what was the most worrying part, only she was making a sort of a low mewling sound, a sound like she was in pain, and weakening from it. She wouldn't feed for a whole night and day. So Mother asked Marie Walsh from up around the corner to drive them in her car as far as Nenagh to the doctor.

The one on the desk at the doctor's was a lightning bitch. Wanting to know had they an appointment. Telling them they had to have an appointment. Mother had screamed at her that she hadn't even a phone, how was she meant to make appointments, her child was sick, where was the doctor? But the one just wrinkled up her nose and said to take a seat. And to calm down. Mother said the one was lucky she had Saoirse in her arms, or she'd have fucking knocked her out. There's nothing in the world worse than being told to calm down when you're up to ninety.

There was a good few meelie-mawlies in the waiting room, and only one seat free, and Mother hadn't wanted to sit in it, because then there'd be people either side of them, looking down at Saoirse, spitting their dirty germs on her. There was a tinker lady on the end seat and she stood and told Mother to sit, and she told all the other people to shove down along and to give the lady space, she had a sick child, proper sick, not like any of them. Now, girl, she'd said, and she'd bent down low so that her mouth was at Mother's ear. Don't worry one bit. And the tinker lady, whose skin was lined like the inside of a tree trunk, whose gnarled hands were heavy with rings, touched her thin lips to Saoirse's forehead and reached for one of her little hands, gently freeing it from inside the blanket Mother had her swaddled in, and she opened Saoirse's hand to examine her palm and said, Missus, this child will live a long, long life, and she'll be a pride to you in everything she does. And Mother was drawing a breath to tell the next part of the story when Saoirse cried out, a shocking cry of sudden cramping pain.

BLOOD

There was blood.

A small streak, bright red, and another trickle following. Mother and Nana were at the bathroom door. Well? Well? There's blood. Blood? Oh, holy Jesus. Can we come in? And they did, and they all three looked down at the place where the bloodstain was, Saoirse stretching out the fabric from herself, bending down low as though to smell it, though she didn't know why its smell seemed important, or how she'd tell one smell from another, but all she could smell anyway was something like the lakeshore, an earthy, mineral smell of water and reed and ancient rock. All these mad thoughts, and her baby's life seeping from her.

Chris was outside the door somehow. How had he known to come? Maybe it was just good fortune, good timing, God directing things, or a guardian angel, or her father, or some magic left on her by a tinker lady in a doctor's waiting room, and she could hear him saying, We'll go on in, so, come on and we'll go on in. I'll bet you it's nothing, this often happens to dams in calf, this is only a bit of excess, and Mother and Nana both shouted at him to shut up, to shut his face, to turn the car in the name of fuck and be ready to go. Poor Chris. Mother and Nana screamed at him the whole way in. Slow down, speed up, go handy, don't brake so hard, come on will you?

They were either side of her in the back seat, turned towards her, too close, but she couldn't say that. Have you a pain now? Can you feel anything below? Do you think you're bleeding still? Good girl. It'll be grand. What will be will be, Nana said, and Mother told her to shut up, never to say that again, that stupid fucking bullshit, if we all lived that way we'd all be dead. And Nana laughed and said, Ah, now. Now, now.

Saoirse felt herself laughing through her fear. She felt herself moving through the hospital doors and across a vast cold expanse of floor, following a kind-faced scrubbed lady, who was making soft, placatory noises, calling her dear, and lovey, and she felt Nana behind her, and Mother, but the lady told them to stay there, to wait, and the lady steered her along a short corridor to a room with a bed and a curtain and she told her to take off her skirt and her underwear, to sit up on the bed, and the lady's hands were gloved and sure in their coldness on her body and she moved across Saoirse's stomach a round metal machine and she said, Listen, lovey, listen, and the lady was smiling, and Saoirse listened, and above her own pounding heartbeat she heard through a tinny speaker at her shoulder the sweet pulsing drumbeat of life. And with the onrush of her relief all of her regret was washed away.

ENGAGEMENT

Chris got engaged.

One damp day Nana sloshed into the kitchen doorway and stood shaking her umbrella back into the yard. She didn't turn to tell them the news: it was as though she hoped to subvert the truth of her words by saying them in the wrong direction. Chris is after getting involved with a one from town. A right-looking apparition. He says they're getting married. He brought her out to the house before I knew a thing about it.

She was still shaking her umbrella hard. Her back was quivering with the effort, her headscarf's maroon peak waving from side to side. Mary, what are you saying? Mother was standing now and her hand was on Nana's elbow, as though to spin her around. Did you not hear me? When she turned her eyes were red-rimmed and sunken a little in her pale face; she looked as though she'd been crying for a long time. My fool above is after getting himself tangled up with a townie one and he marched in last night late dragging her behind him, a little scrawny number in a jumper and trousers she got in a jumble sale I'd say, you wouldn't believe the cut of her, Eileen, and he grinning back to his two ears like a jackass, and he told me she was his *fiancée*. Even the way he said it sounded foolish. *Fiancée*. Nana dragged the word out and deepened her voice in a miserable parody of her youngest son's voice. She sobbed then, and put her arms out to Mother, who embraced her like a woman putting her arms around a crying child, and Saoirse could see from her seat at the table that Mother's eyes, too, were filled with tears.

After they'd settled themselves with cups of tea and cigarettes Mother asked for more details about the betrothal. Tell me now, Mary, who exactly is she? Doreen *Williams*? That's a funny name. I've never heard of anyone called Williams. Not in Nenagh, anyway. Maybe she's Protestant? Oh, Lord bless us, Nana said, don't even joke about it. What part of town is she from exactly? Nana told her and Mother declared that part of town to be full of bowsies. What did she look like again? Like a one that had one leg shorter than the other but had it fixed but then never learnt to walk straight afterwards. Kind of bandy-legged and crooked in the back, mousy and very low in the speech, like a one that was afraid of her life to say anything, but they caught me on the hop rightly, I can tell you, and not even Paudie knew a thing about this big romance, though I don't know how that's possible.

Nana rose and sighed expansively and dragged herself away to the bathroom to recompose herself. Mother pulled hard at her fag. Jesus Christ, Chris, she whispered, as though He and not Saoirse were sitting across from her. Jesus Christ almighty.

FOREHEAD

News of Saoirse's pregnancy had a terrible effect on Oonagh Jones.

She was Oisín's girlfriend now and the rumours that he was the father were ruinous to her unsullied ideals of romance, the sense of sacredness she felt about her first love. She got off the school bus on the first day of the revelation with her face tear-streaked and her sinuses stuffed with snot. She could hardly breathe through her catarrh of grief and rage.

Oonagh Jones started to shout at the entrance to the estate. Saoirse was at home, having ended her school career the week before, or taken a hiatus as she'd sworn to her mother. A small band of embarrassed followers trailed in Oonagh's wake, glancing nervously at each other. Her shouts spread in a wave of febrile pitch before her, across all the small tidy lawns and flowerbeds, into all the houses of the small development, to the ears of all the people who were home, drawing them to their windows, and out to their doorsteps.

You dirty fucking whore, Saoirse Aylward. You cunt. You'd better fucking tell everyone it wasn't my boyfriend that knocked you up. You fucking smelly bitch. He wouldn't touch you with a bargepole. Come out, you fucking slut. But Saoirse didn't go out. She stood in the shallow bay of the front window and watched as her mother strode along the concrete driveway to the footpath where Oonagh Jones stood, alone now, because her minions had scattered to the safety of their homes, and Oonagh's face was ruby red and glistening with tears and snot as she screamed, I'll kill you! And Saoirse watched as her mother arched her spine backwards and sprang herself forward again so that her forehead met the bridge of Oonagh Jones's nose, and Oonagh Jones fell backwards onto the damp tarmacadam, her landing softened by her schoolbag, her school skirt bunched up at her waist and her bare white legs wide open to the world.

Saoirse felt sad for Oonagh Jones. She felt sad in that moment for anyone in the world who didn't have a mother like hers. A mother who was standing now above her quarry like a prizefighter in a swell of victory, looking slowly left and right as if to challenge with her silent stare any comers, who was looking at the windows and doorways of her neighbours' houses through dark eyes flashing with anger and wild strength. Nana blessed herself and tutted and watched as Mother helped Oonagh up from the ground and smoothed her jumper and skirt, and held a tissue to her bleeding nose. She heard Mother say, Hold your head straight. Go on home now and don't ever roar into my house like that again. Don't ever call my child those dirty names again. Sure you won't? That's a good girl. And Oonagh Jones shook her wounded head, and Nana shook her head too, in fearful wonder and pride in the widow of her firstborn son.

RECONSTRUCTION

Jim Gildea rolled slowly along the avenue.

Oonagh Jones's father had called him. Oonagh had tried to stop him. She wanted it to be over and forgotten about; she'd rung Oisín on her new mobile phone and he'd sworn on his life and her life and all their parents' lives that he'd never had sex with Saoirse Aylward. She'd given him a hand job once and that had been it, and that was nearly a year ago. Jim gathered the belligerents at the scene of the incident. The westering sun was tired and red; the evening was getting cold. Come on, he said, show me what happened. What, like, a *reconstruction*? Oonagh Jones wrinkled her face and avoided Eileen Aylward's flashing eyes. That's *stupid*. Oonagh's father was standing by the transformer box that was set on the edge of the footpath at the bottom of the hill. He shouted over now: Jim! Hey, Jim! What kind of bolloxology is this? But Jim ignored him.

Now, ladies. Here's what we'll do. We'll establish all the facts quickly. Show me now exactly what happened. Saoirse and Nana watched through the open sash of the bay window as Mother backed down the yard and started again towards Oonagh, who was standing roughly where she'd been standing when she'd delivered her shrieked volleys and had been silenced by Mother's hard forehead. She was there, Jim, where she is now, and she was roaring every kind of dog's abuse in the yard at us, accusing my daughter of all sorts, and using the most foul language. Then she threatened to kill me, or Saoirse, or both of us, I'm not sure, so I gave her one quick wallop into the face.

Jim pushed his lips outwards contemplatively and scratched first his fleshy chin and then his belly. What did you wallop her with, Eileen? My forehead, Jim. He looked at Oonagh, who looked back at him with eyes as wide as the eyes of a birthing cow. Is that all true? More or less, said Oonagh, and her hand went reflexively to the small dark patch where Mother's frontal bone had met her nasal bone. I had a bad nosebleed. She sniffed.

Jim said nothing. He opened the boot of his car and rummaged for a few seconds before drawing from it two pairs of handcuffs. Right. Mrs Aylward, I'm arresting you on suspicion of assault. Miss Jones, I'm arresting you on suspicion of making threats to kill. Turn around now the two of ye until I put these onto ye. Oonagh's father was walking white-faced towards them, his hands raised. Mother was smiling at Jim. Oonagh was crying and making a moaning sound. Nana laughed softly as Jim said: Or ye can admit that there was a pair of ye in it, shake hands, and promise to keep the peace. And they did.

That Jim Gildea is the best of men, said Nana, as he drove away. God bless him and keep him.

WEDDING

She toughed it out, anyway.

Doreen, the timid interloper from some dark recess of town, from people of no account in Nana's estimation, though she made a good show of welcoming them and of pleasant familiarity with them, walked the aisle of the Church of the Holy Spirit, in a simple white dress, apologetically pretty on her father's arm. Paudie stood still and straight-backed beside his brother, who gazed with a curious, wide-eyed expression along the aisle at his approaching fate, at the unexpected life that was being escorted towards him through the whirling organ song, through the thin phalanx of family and friends, some smiling, some grave, most of those on the groom's side laying their eyes for the first time on the bride. Nana stood pursed of lip and damp of eye, her opposite number on the other front pew assuming a similar aspect, both women's chins raised in defiance of the other's reservations, neither woman giving an inch of ground in the pitched battle of forced pleasantness and nuptial bonhomie.

They had an old-fashioned wedding breakfast in Jim Barry's pub in Newtown, at tables ranged along the lounge in rows, Chris and Paudie and the bride and her sister and the two mothers and the new father-in-law installed at a top table set perpendicular to the lines of cousins and aunts and uncles and friends. Saoirse placed herself at the most distant corner from the chief celebrants, sensitive to Nana's embarrassment about her condition, as she referred to it, and Mother sat beside her smoking, smoking, talking to no one, making a humming sound now and again, nudging Saoirse and pointing with her cigarette's business end at various of the wedding party, saying in a sharp whisper, I know that waster, he loses his wages in the shop every week, I've seen that lanky one around the town dragging five or six children behind her, look at the big one above near the top table, the cut of her and she taking up two seats, and then to the phantom Chris, not this new Chris, who sat impossibly married across the wedding lounge in ill-fitting splendour, but the Chris who'd stood and shaken as he proposed to Mother all those years ago, his hand held out beseeching, his heart sitting raw and invisible in the palm of it, Oh, Chris, what are you after doing?

As Saoirse returned from the Ladies, in the noisy lull between the end of feasting and the start of speeches, she saw her mother's lonely back and thin arms with their sharp elbows and felt a surge of sadness and love so strong that it winded her. When Paudie stood and told the room that his brother was the best friend a man could have, that he wished he could be half the man his little brother was, Saoirse felt her mother's hand on hers and heard her softly saying, It'll be all right. We'll all be all right. Won't we?

ENDURANCE

It's just not going to work.

Nana told Saoirse and Mother that she'd tried her damnedest with her but she just had to admit that it wasn't going to work out between herself and Doreen. Nana regretted her easy acquiescence to the arrangement that Chris and Doreen would set up home in the farmhouse. *What got into me at all? I should have known it wouldn't work.* She took off cleaning without telling me, pulling all my ware out of my presses and spraying stuff into them and a face on her like she was cleaning a dirty toilet, and she wanted to know when I last had a *spring-clean.* I ask you. This is a farm, I said to her, and you're a farmer's wife, and do you know what she said? Do you know what the little mouse found it inside in herself to squeak to me? She said, Well, it's not *much* of a farm, now, is it?

And she has a pure gom made out of Chris. He looks at her doe-eyed, with this kind of a foolish smile, and he only grins when she blackens me, and I hear her blackening me. Every day she's at it. I let on to be deaf as a stone, you see, and I make her roar when she's talking to me, the way she thinks then that when she's reading me to Chris abroad in the hallway or out in the yard that I can't hear her, but I hear every word. Your mother hates me, she says. I can do nothing right. We have to get out of here. I want my own house. And my poor fool placating her away. And then the noises they make at night! Oh, Lord save us, I never heard the like of it. I lie there thinking, Is that my son? Is that really the quiet decent boy I reared, making those noises? And she screeching out of her like a one being killed from the pleasure of it. Well for her, I suppose. It was an endurance in my day. You said your prayers until it was over and then you prayed again.

Please, Mary, Mother said, stop it, please. And they all three of them laughed through the disturbing thought of the terrible noises travelling along the old house's mildewed hallway, through its stout and ancient doors to Nana's prickling perfect ears, of the new wife easy in her throes, of the husband in his disbelief that such pleasure could exist, giving vent to all their ecstasies.

There's only one thing for it, Mother said one day to Nana, as the end of Saoirse's pregnancy approached, as her swollen body pushed its bounds to bursting. You'll have to come and live with us.

Nana was quiet for a while, and her eyes took on a dreamy sheen, as though she were imagining this new life and all it might entail, before she said, Yes. I will.

ROOM

The extension was Mother's idea.

Nana approved. Saoirse and the child will need more space. We'll get Mickey Briars to knock the wall and dig out the foundations and lay the concrete, she said, and sure after that it's only a matter of laying block on top of block. Chris and Paudie will do that for us no problem.

They will in my eye, said Mother. Nana took a snout for a while, allowing the kitchen to fill with cigarette smoke and silent resentment. Eventually, Mother elaborated on her opposition to Nana's plan. Look, Mary. I'm sorry now. But I'm not having those gobshites building me a half-arsed crooked room that'll fall in on top of the child.

Nana pursed her lips and pushed them outwards, working her dentures loose with her tongue so that Saoirse could see the pink-white spit-shined rim of them protruding for a moment. Nana only did that when she needed to stop herself from speaking. I've seen their handiwork, Mary. Don't I live with it every day in this kitchen? Scrap timber and fucking plywood held together with spit and bullshit. I know they're your sons and I love them dearly too, but they haven't a straight line between them.

Nana had to concede the point. But still they hadn't the price of an extension and that was all there was to it. Mother sat one evening later that week at the kitchen table with a ruler and pencil and a sheet of paper that nearly covered the entire table, and the sheet was taped in place at each corner. There was a library book open on the sheet, and Mother had her glasses on and she was copying from what looked like a diagram of a house onto the paper, and after four hours or maybe five she shouted, YES! and she sat back in her chair and lit a cigarette.

Saoirse wanted badly to see what she had drawn. She moved silently from the window seat where she'd been sitting, watching, cradling her bump, dozing occasionally, and into the kitchen. She stood behind her mother and looked at the tidy drawing she had done, of their house in plan, and behind it she'd drawn a square addition with a smaller square in one corner and the letters WC inside the square. I know you're there behind me, Mother said, without turning. This is for you and the baby. A bigger bedroom with its own toilet. A bit of privacy. And that's all that was said that night.

The next day a battered van pulled into the yard and a man got out, a tall, weather-beaten man with red cheeks and blue overalls and heavy black boots and on his head a black beret with a harp on it, and on the harp a double F, and Saoirse wondered what the Fs were for. The man looked from her face to her bump and back to her face and said, Where's your mother?

MASON

The man was Mickey Briars.

He knocked walls, dug trenches and poured concrete over two nonstop days. Now, he said, from the kitchen door, at the start of the third day. I need ye women to come out here. Anything I tell ye I'm only telling ye once. If ye can't follow me that's hard lines. And so Saoirse and Mother followed him to the back garden. The tangled country over which Saoirse had in her childhood presided was reduced now to a narrow enclave. A pile of blocks had been delivered by truck the previous evening and it stood taller than the red-faced builder. He straightened himself and pushed his chest out and started slowly to speak. These here, he said, pointing at the blocks, are blocks. And these here, he said, pointing at an array of implements by his feet, are a mortar board, a trowel, a level, a line, pegs, and a measure. Now, which of ye will be doing the block laying?

I will, said Mother. Right. Come on over here so and watch me closely while I lay the first row of the far wall. Then you can lay the second row on top of it, and I'll stay in case you balls it up. Then I must be on my way which or whether, good or bad. And he showed her how to use the mortar, how to keep her line, to cut the edge blocks clean, how and where to insert ties.

All that morning Mother and the bereted builder toiled,

him bent to the task of mortaring and laying block after block along a straight stringed line, in two rows with a small cavity between them, and Mother bent herself close beside him, and listened while the builder pointed and explained, and he watched as she laid mortar with the trowel and placed a block onto it, and he nodded his approval and Saoirse heard him say, Good girl, begod, good girl you are. You have it, you have it, God bless your hands you do.

He left. Mother and Nana pushed their bodies to the limit of their endurance, working and working day after day until the light was gone and the pile of blocks reduced in height as the walls of the room grew higher, and when the line of blocks was at their chests they used a blue bandstand that the builder had left, and the three women between them carried blocks from the pile, Mother telling Saoirse to stop, to mind her own business, as they laid the blocks clean along the plumb line onto the mortar, and they lintelled the window-space, and eventually they reached the line of the roof.

Now, Mother said, Here's the tricky part. But we're fucking doing it. And the next day they did. By the end of the third week the walls stood, tied and insulated and nearly straight, the roof was on, and the neighbours to a woman were amazed.

NATIVITY

She was born.

Seventeen years and ten months after her mother, after a half-day of labour, she came crying into the world. Her grandmother and great-grandmother attended her birth, despite the snooty midwife and the shooing nurses. Her great-uncle Paudie drove the carful of generations home, slowly, as Saoirse once was driven the same roads home, and she kissed her daughter's face as she was kissed. The world at once expanded outwards and compressed itself inwards, the universe now was a single unit of being, seven pounds and one bare ounce of eggshell bones and downy skin and purblind eyes in perfect sockets, and there was silence in the car but for the soft, probing sounds of her, and the occasional instruction from Mother or from Nana about her head, support her head, slow down, Paudie, and now and then an impatient honk from the cortège of cars and vans that snaked for a country mile behind them.

Father unknown. Yes, that's what you can write on your form, and you can take your form then and stick it in your pipe and smoke it for all I care. Nana repeated what she'd said to the girl at her granddaughter's bedside as she'd sat with her hand on the edge of her great-granddaughter's hospital cradle, and they laughed again at the memory of the woman's blood-less lips and prissy face, the way she'd looked at Saoirse, down her nose literally, down along her snobby nose. They must be fecking used to it by now, surely. Anyway, if they're not it's all idle, the way the world is gone these days. What's left to be shocked about in this day and age? Our dear Lord and Saviour is two thousand years old, and His Father's world is the same world it always was for all it's changed, everyone still judging everyone else the same way He was judged.

Neighbours came and were kind and congratulatory. A pile of outfits grew against the sitting-room wall. A row of cards lined the mantelpiece. Some of them contained money and Mother stacked the notes behind the clock, logging the donors and the amounts. The vexed question of fatherhood was studiously avoided, but Saoirse heard through the opened sash of the front window a neighbour speculating at the far side of the cherry blossom, Is it young Rahilly is the father? and she thought of Oisín, his soft palm in hers, the redness in his cheeks, the fire in his eyes as he begged her to let him go further, imploring almost to the point of tears, and the pleasure his desperation gave her, in the pain she knew she was causing him. And she imagined then the singer, sitting somewhere, sweeping his hair from his eyes, strumming a guitar and leaning over it to plot his chords and words, humming some nascent melody to himself, oblivious in his burgeoning, glistening world to his daughter, who reached upwards towards a blur of shining love.

LOVE

S he hadn't been prepared for the force of it.
  She couldn't quite contain it for the first while. It was as
though its magnitude was too great for her being, that it
couldn't be marshalled within her thin frame so that her
actions were outside of herself: crying for no reason; snapping
at Mother and Nana for silly things; pacing the room barefoot
while the baby slept. She imagined constantly all sorts of terrible scenarios: fires and kidnapping and sinkholes opening
underneath the house. A news report showed an explosion in
some war-torn place and a group of men lifting a child's bloodied body above their heads and she cried for hours.

Mother and Nana understood. It was familiar to them.
They spent as much time staring at the baby as Saoirse did,
cooing and shushing and singing all sorts of sweet songs and
lullabies. They didn't tell her to cop on as she would have
expected but were solicitous and ever present; like two adults
watching a child carry a full glass of water across a room, they
were ready at any moment to step in and take the load to obvi-
ate the risk of spillage, of slippage, of something going wrong.
They praised her as a child would be praised for colouring
within the lines or drawing a pretty picture: You're one great
little mother, Saoirse; Lord, you're taking to it like a duck to

water; now, there, you have the hang of it, now you have it, you're a great girl.

A clicking feeling of sharp momentary pain travelled from the top of her head to the ends of her toes as the baby clamped its gums around her and started to suck, subsiding into a warm, pleasant, dragging sensation, a feeling of rightness and relief. Sitting in a shaft of warm light that shone through lines of rain on the window as Nana sat by the stove calling slowly name after name and Mother responding with no, or maybe, or fuck no, it seemed so unimportant a thing to do, weirdly redundant, to put a label on this perfect thing, and so narrow her down to a single small collection of letters that made particular sounds that evoked a certain sensation or a certain way of being or a type of person, a person who was from a certain place or would have a prescribed set of facets and would do certain things.

She's a week old tomorrow, Nana said. We're gone to the dogs at this stage. How is it at all we can't pick a name for her? And she went on with her litany: Bridget? NO! Theresa? NO! Winifred? NO! Marie? NO! Annie? NO! Olive? NO! Okay. Well, what about ye two? Ye haven't an idea between ye. Why is this being left to me?

Late that evening, on his way home from silage-making for a farmer in Labasheeda, Paudie called in and said, Isn't she a pearl? And Pearl she was.

SALLY

One bright midday a sleek silver car pulled up at the kerb. Jesus Christ, said Mother. It's Sally. She crossed the room into the porch and opened the front door to the pretty brown-haired lady that Saoirse had last seen in Youghalarra graveyard one drizzly anniversary morning years before. She had lost none of her prettiness but gained a softness to her features and a light crow's foot either side of her kind eyes. Sally sat and stared at Pearl for a long time. Even as she told them about her life, lecturing at a university in Dublin, and her husband, who managed a fund, whatever that meant, she kept her eyes on Pearl's face, and Pearl lay gazing serenely back at her.

Sally asked Saoirse if she was happy to be a mother. And Saoirse looked into the woman's eyes and said she was. There's no reason in the world why being a mother should hold you back, Saoirse. In fact, it'll make you all the stronger, and better able to square up to the world and to fight your corner. Always fight, Saoirse, won't you? For yourself and for her. Don't ever allow yourself to be trampled on. Saoirse looked past her visitor and saw that Mother and Nana were both looking at her solemnly, and they were nodding their agreement with Sally's words.

Sally smiled then, and asked if she could pick Pearl up, and when she did she held her to her chest and lowered her face to

Pearl's face and Saoirse saw a tear fall onto Pearl's rosy cheek and shimmer there a moment, and Sally said, Our daddies will look after her, Saoirse, you can be sure of that. Saoirse felt suddenly a curious pang of an emotion she couldn't quite identify; guilt, she supposed, was closest to it, for having been born the day she'd been born, a little bit early, so that her father's fate and that of Sally's father collided on the bend at the end of the Esker Line. And worse again the guilt she felt at her own lack of sadness, while this woman's heart, it seemed, had never mended.

Mother came back in from seeing Sally off with a bag in her hand of gifts, expensive outfits from Mothercare and Brown Thomas, and a card at the bottom of the bag with a picture on its front of a baby in a crib with a white winged angel hovering behind it, and inside she'd written, *to Saoirse and baby Pearl, may you always have peace*. God help us, said Mother. Poor Sally. All she ever wanted was a baby of her own. And all the money in the world couldn't buy her one.

And Saoirse felt again a sharp flare of guilt as she thought of the rainy drunken night, the singer's sour-sweet lips, the seconds of blurry fumbling that the universe had somehow sublimated into this precious incarnation, this miracle of blood and bone and flesh.

PRODIGAL

Everyone gets that word wrong, you know.

Kit Gladney had a cross look on her face, an unfamiliar expression on such a serene woman. The word prodigal doesn't mean returned. It means profligate, wasteful. In the Gospel of Luke the son was wasteful and extravagant and went around the place acting like a little lord and when he hadn't an arse left in his trousers he came back to his father's house and the father welcomed him with open arms. The fatted calf was killed in his honour. The prodigal son was returned; he wasn't a prodigal son *because* he returned.

Yerra, now, said Nana. If you're going to let that upset you, dear friend, you'll be cribbing a long time. If your grandson is going to disappear for years the very same way his mother did, and then drag back up that hill without a warning, he's going to have to resign himself to being called a few names. Sticks and stones. Kit Gladney, who was well up on her eighties and a good half a decade older than Nana, ignored her imperiously, and went on with her lecture. All I'm saying is I'm sick of every Tom, Dick and Harry congratulating me on the prodigal returned, just like the time long 'go when Moll came back from England and we had years of it, we had, every nose in ten parishes being poked in the top of the door and ha-ha, ha-ha thee, look out, the prodigal returned, the prodigal returned, and now it's the same thing again with Joshua. THREE TIMES between Knockagowny and here, not a mile of a walk, I had to listen to it. Tom Rock going along beside me on his bicycle, Hello, Kit, did I hear the prodigal returned? I nearly pushed him off, so I did.

Anyway, hand me over that child until I have a good measure of her. And she angled herself outwards from the table so that Saoirse could place Pearl in her lap, happy and well-fed Pearl, on the edge of sleep, looking through her half-closed milky eyes at all the happy moving forms above her, soaking through her translucent skin all their adoration. Oh, lads, oh, lads, that takes me back. I remember my Moll when she was after being fed; she always had that glow about her, you could feel the happiness coming off of her in waves. Is she winded? And Saoirse said she wasn't yet, but a bare few taps was all it ever took, and Kit Gladney, whose heart had been broken again and again and whose mended heart was still pure and full of love, hefted the little body gracefully from her lap to her shoulder and three expert taps of her dear fingers later Pearl burped loudly and Mother and Saoirse and Nana cheered, and Kit Gladney declared that she'd never lost it.

I'll send them down tomorrow, so. Honey, his girlfriend's name is. Wait until ye see her.

HONEY

Joshua Elmwood was a few years older than Saoirse.

She remembered when his father, Alexander, had died, in a car accident, like her own father. She'd been seven or maybe eight. Mother and Nana had cried all day. She remembered them saying how beautiful a man he'd been in every way. Beautiful seemed a strange word to use for a man. She remembered him at mass, with his wife on one side of him and his son on the other, how he'd towered above them. She remembered the brightness of his smile, how different he'd looked from the other fathers, how gentle he'd seemed. She remembered feeling sad that she'd never see him again, his stooped back and huge hands and kind eyes, the hat he always wore as he walked through the village with his wife and son and his wife's parents, when most men wore peaked caps if they bothered with headwear at all. She could see now through the proxy of his living son the inherited beauty that Mother and Nana had lamented. She remembered jokes in school about Josh Elmwood's colour and the shock his mother and father must have gotten when he came out white, and how it was usually the other way round, ha-ha.

And here he was, this infamous boy who'd been in trouble over drugs, it was said by the most ungenerous of the rumour-mongers, who hadn't the goodness or the decency of his father,

God rest him, who'd disappeared the very same way his mother did years ago, and, lads, doesn't breeding break out through the eye of a cat? What's in the blood is in the blood, nothing can be done. Because the very same as his mother landed back to the townland of Knockagowny above the village with a Black man, the lad was after arriving back, after the bones of four years of absence, with a Black girl. It was comical, really, the gossipers declared with glee. The Gladneys and their predilections. The Gladneys and their wild adventures. But anyway. What harm?

Nana couldn't understand it. Tell me now again who this girl is. Are you Alexander's daughter? Or his sister? Are you one of the Elmwoods? She was raising her voice and enunciating her words slowly as though unsure whether the visitor spoke English. Mother was nearly shouting now. Jesus Christ almighty, Mary, will you please stop saying that? Will you please for the love of God leave the girl alone? She's Joshua's girlfriend. That's all you need to know. Now SHUT UP! But Nana wouldn't let it go. Well, how come then she looks so like our Alexander, God love him and God rest him? And the girl spoke then, smiling at Nana, leaning towards her from where she sat at the dining table in front of the window, saying, slowly and clearly, in a soft London accent, I'm Honey Bartlett. Alexander was my godfather.

Godfather? Nana screeched. Yerra, that makes no sense at all.

REVENANT

Honey's father, Syd, had brought them back from London. He'd stayed a few days with Kit and her daughter, Moll, Josh's mother. It was like something out of a film, Kit said, the way they appeared at the halfway stile and I looked through the window and I was sure and certain 'twas Alexander risen from the dead and coming up the lane towards me, and then I saw Honey and Josh behind her, and, well, I don't know how to describe the feeling. Heaven, I suppose. Like Heaven. I'll never forget Moll's face when she came in the door, and Syd and Joshua and Honey and myself sitting at the table having a bit to eat, the very same as if we'd sat together at that table every evening of our lives. I had them told for sport just to act real casual, not to make anything of the situation when she arrived in. But it was a pantomime. She stood in the doorway looking and looking. Then she put her hands up over her face and took them away again to see were they still there, and none of us said a word until for a finish Joshua stood up and said, Well, Mam, and the spell was broken. Oh, thank God, she said, over and over again. Thank God, thank God. You're home. And she told him there and then he was never going anywhere again, but I can't see how she'll be able to enforce that proscription.

Honey decided she'd stay awhile, didn't you, love? And the

girl smiled and nodded, and Nana wondered aloud how that would work. How's that going to work? she shouted across the room, from the corner of the couch where she was cradling Pearl. Saoirse wondered if Nana had suffered more strokes and hadn't let on, or maybe didn't know. She seemed to be having more trouble than usual grasping things, simple things like the relationships between the people being spoken about and who were sitting here in living flesh before her. She remembered reading a novel about the lives of the various passengers on a bus and one of them was an old man who knew he was having a series of minor strokes because he could feel things loosening and popping in his head and he couldn't focus his eyes and his ears rang constantly and he had spells of weakness and confusion but he was able to mask his symptoms well, and she felt a stab of panic at the idea of a world without Nana.

Honey told them about how her father had visited the spot at Ballywilliam where his childhood friend Alexander had died. He'd knelt and kissed the tarmacadam and cried. And Saoirse remembered how Mother and Nana always blessed themselves at the bend of the road where her father had been killed, and again she felt a pang of guilt at her absence of grief, for never having knelt there and cried.

KINGPIN

Paudie was arrested again.

It was different this time. Paudie was different. He'd become, it seemed, something bigger than they'd realized: he was a man to be feared in reality and not just by reputation, a man who caused things to happen and commanded things. He was far more now than a useful fool who'd put his barn at the disposal of shadowy strangers or who drove fugitives at night from safehouse to safehouse. His face was shown on television, a story appeared about him in a Sunday newspaper, the parish closed itself in around the Aylwards and the word went around that nobody was to talk to reporters, that all strangers were to be suspected of being Special Branch unless they could be vouched for, that unfamiliar faces were to be given no welcome. Saoirse felt a strange gratitude towards Paudie: it was as if he'd sacrificed his freedom for the safety of her daughter, as if he'd contrived this situation so that their small house would have a sanctity attached to it, would become rarefied, would have a squad car close by at all times, driving slowly up and down the boreen to the farmhouse and past it to Paudie's little renovated cottage, or in and out of the estate, as though some information about Paudie would somehow become apparent to them if they drove the area enough times or looked through enough good people's windows.

A man had been shot in Ennis, an hour or so of a drive away but close enough *to his base of operations* for Paudie to have done it, or organized it, or even ordered it. The solicitor who'd been appointed to represent him had paid a visit to Nana out of courtesy, and to have a look at the farmhouse and the outbuildings, to ensure that the damage that had been done during the police search was put right. He explained to Nana that Paudie could be held for a long time, that he'd been denied bail by the Special Criminal Court, that the Special Criminal Court wasn't in fact a court of law or justice but an insidious mechanism created and used for state terrorism, to allow for non-jury trials. Show trials, Mrs Aylward. It's a travesty of justice. But none of that talk was any help to Nana, whose son was gone from her, or to Chris, who shook with anger and worry.

Honey and Josh came almost daily down the hillside now. Pearl seemed to recognize their faces: she'd point at them and smile when they arrived. Honey was fascinated by the situation. She told a story about her father being arrested in the eighties, about how he'd hidden in the attic of a neighbour's house, and had only revealed himself when the police had started to break their neighbours' doors down with a battering ram. Nana was impressed by this. Imagine that, she said. Imagine. Ye poor misfortunes. Haven't people the same troubles no matter what?

CONFLICT

Jim Gildea called in one day, out of uniform.

He was wearing a grey raincoat against the showery weather and he was holding a flat cap in his big hands, the way he'd have been holding his Garda hat if he'd been on duty. God bless all here, Jim said, in a way that struck Saoirse as very old-fashioned but that felt natural and heartfelt the way he said it. He looked from the porch into the sitting room and through the archway to the kitchen, logging the faces looking back at him, nodding briefly at each one: Saoirse, Mother, Nana, Kit, Josh, Honey, and, in a red travel cot in the middle of the sitting room, Pearl, examining her fingers with gurgling wonder. He smiled down at her.

Nana wouldn't look at him and insisted on addressing him as Sergeant. Paudie was still on remand but the surveillance operation was over. Saoirse missed the feeling of security the squad car had given her, and Nana, she knew, had quite enjoyed the elevation of it all, having allowed herself the notion that her son was at the vanguard of a holy struggle, that he was, in his incarceration, a living martyr.

Who have I in it? Jim asked, smiling at Honey. She looked at him, confused at the construction. Josh answered for her: This is Honey Bartlett. Nice to meet you, Honey, Jim said. Nana was bristling, moving around in her seat, as if preparing to jump from it and attack poor Jim. Well, Sergeant, well? What do you want with us? Are you going to start flinging things around the way your buddies did above in my house? The place was solid destroyed. Poor Doreen got a terrible shock. The girl not married a wet week and those bastards terrorizing her in her new home.

I know, Mary. They go overboard sometimes. It was all put back right, though, wasn't it? It was in my eye put back right. And don't you pretend you're not one of them. I am, said Jim. And I won't apologize. People are being killed, Mary, innocent people, parents of children and children of parents. For what reason? None in the world, only pure solid madness. Nana's face was red now and her eyes filled with tears. When news had broken of the most recent murder she'd been upset for days, had retreated into silent, fervent rosaries. She tried to hold her toughness now.

I suppose you're going to try to tell me, Sergeant, that Paudie had something to do with that, and he inside in prison when it happened? Everyone looked at Jim. Pearl cooed and coughed sweetly. I only came to check in, Mary. To see if ye were all okay. Well, don't worry yourself about us, Sergeant. We're well able to look after ourselves. Go on now. And Nana waved him away. Before he left, he smiled again at Pearl and then at Saoirse. She's a beautiful baby, Jim said.

SACRAMENTS

It was Nana's idea to ask Josh and Honey to be Pearl's godparents.

Ask that lovely boy and girl. They're here to stay, I'd say, and if they're not, what odds? It's a small world now. They seemed touched and a little embarrassed. Father Cotter agreed but said that he'd have to confirm Honey. Josh was indignant on Honey's behalf when this information was relayed from the parochial house, complaining about the patriarchy and infantilization, but Nana, whom they'd thought was asleep in her chair in the corner, suddenly said, Ah, shut up, young Elmwood, in the name of God. What will it harm the girl to say *I do* a few times to keep Father Cotter happy? More in your line now to be reading the barber that was meant to cut your hair. Was his scissors blunt? Josh smiled at Nana, and she smiled back at him, because they were uncommonly fond of one another, and it was agreed that Honey would be confirmed at mass the following Sunday, and that she'd receive communion, and would stand for Pearl at her post-mass baptism.

Won't that be a big day for you now, lovey? said Nana. Getting your confirmation and your communion and then becoming a godparent all in the same hour. Lord God, ye young people don't do things by halves, and that is for sure. All a rush and everything backwards, of course. Backwards? said

Saoirse. Ya, backwards. Having babies before ye're married and being confirmed before ye get communion, and wanting the whole world to change itself around for ye. I don't know. Where will it all end?

I don't know, Nana, where it's all going to end for us, but it's going to end for you in the fucking county home if you don't shut up. Nana straightened up in her chair, and scrabbled around for her glasses and narrowed her sparkling eyes. Oh, faith. The county home? Well, it may surprise you to hear, madam, that I'd be quite happy to remove myself to the county home if it meant I was treated with a modicum of respect, and not spoken to like I was a bould child, by a bould child. I'm a bould child, am I? You are, said Nana. You were gave too much rope always, and it was no wonder that you got yourself tied up in all sorts of knots. You're a fucking old cow, Nana, said Saoirse, and Nana just smiled, and picked up her *Sacred Heart Messenger*, and opened it ostentatiously.

It was all talk, of course, and none of it meant. Honey told Saoirse later that she loved to listen to these exchanges, to consider where she'd plant her camera if she were to record them, whether she'd use a grip or handheld, whether she'd zoom into the face of each speaker or create a fly-on-the-wall effect. And that Sunday she took her vows for Pearl, who was swaddled in ancient lace, surrounded by love.

NATURE

Josh got a job in a factory in Limerick.

Every weekday morning he waited at the yellow bridge for the early bus. He started at eight and finished at four. He said the factory was like a silent war-zone. The workers sat in long rows assembling parts for computers with soldering irons or with their hands for the simpler operations; the supervisors sat at the heads of each row, and the managers sat behind glass along the top wall in cubicles, venturing out now and then to walk down the lines, looking, checking things with the supervisors, and all the while there were pitched battles being fought. In low mumbles, in passive-aggressive gestures, in fits of sporadic low-level violence, in the forming and splitting and re-forming of cliques and alliances and treaties, a constant state of complex war existed. Supervisors were despised by line workers, who saw them as traitors for being elevated to positions of petty power. Workers from country areas banded together against workers from city estates. Some groups were a mix of both, and those groups were riven by internecine strife. Fights sometimes broke out in the toilets, and a young woman had her nose broken once, but management was universally hated and feared and so a policy of absolute *omertà* was observed among workers.

Josh said he loved the factory, because it was a clear window into unreconstructed human nature. He said that the factory floor was a microcosm of every society, that its arrangements and dynamics and intense stratifications followed a very simple pattern observable everywhere in the world, but he was in the centre of its exposed parts, like a person shrunk and standing inside a cell, witnessing how life itself worked from the inside. Honey smiled as Josh spoke, and looked at him with an expression that seemed to Saoirse to occupy a space between adoration and amusement, like he was a very interesting pet that could do a lot of tricks but was, at the end of the day, an animal, faithful and dumb and incapable of survival without a steady supply of benevolent love.

Honey seemed to Saoirse to exist in a kind of a haze of unreasonable happiness. Everything about this tiny triangle of world between the Gladneys' cottage, and the house where Saoirse and Eileen and Pearl and Nana lived, and the shore of the lake another mile downhill, seemed to interest and delight her. She walked for hours at a time on rainless days with Saoirse and Pearl in her buggy, picnics stowed in Pearl's baby bag alongside her nappies and creams and wipes. She wore an old-fashioned boxy camera around her neck. At the shore of the lake on a calm glistening day she took a photograph of Saoirse as she breastfed Pearl, sitting cross-legged on a bed of shingle. You're so beautiful, she said. You're a natural mother. And Saoirse felt a rush of embarrassed pride, and a distant budding love for this strange girl.

CUT

Pearl was a year on earth.

Mother had a car now, a small hatchback with a kind face and a tired body, and she came home the morning of Pearl's birthday with its boot full of stuffed animals and a giant cake with Pearl's name iced across it framed by a love heart of cream dollops. She covered Pearl's face with kisses as she always did, and Saoirse felt somewhere distant, a vague and amorphous memory of her own face being kissed, of being freshly changed and bounced gently backwards on a bed, and of Mother above her, making these same sonorous loving sounds, kissing her face and stomach. But that memory couldn't be real. No one could remember that far back. But it felt real, for all its blurred edges. She wondered if Mother would deny it, like the memory of the cherry blossom and the long-backed photographer.

The house was filled with women. Mother and Nana and Saoirse and Honey and Kit and Josh's mother, Moll, and Moll's old friend and alleged lover Ellen Jackman, and Doreen, quiet but friendly and no sign about her of the harridan that Nana had made her out to be, and in the centre of all of them, sitting up and trying her best to move around her soft-edged space, grizzling now and then against her cutting buds of teeth, smiling at the rank of women smiling back at her, delighted with and fascinated by all the sounds and smells and shapes and textures of her universe, was Pearl, a perfect little queen, fat with love. Ellen Jackman said: Aren't we the queerest coven that ever stirred a pot? And they all laughed.

Honey had made a film, and it was contained on a video cassette with a white label taped to its side, and on the label was a single word: Love. The film was a present to Pearl, she said, and to the whole family. To everyone here, actually, she said. You're all in it. Oh, Lord, said Nana, look out. But she moved herself as close to the television as she could, and she leant towards it with relish.

Honey had made the film, mostly surreptitiously it seemed, with an ancient 8mm camera, and she'd had the film transferred to video by an old school friend of Josh's in Nenagh. A track of soft piano music played behind the silent scenes as the past year of all their lives spooled out on the screen. Nana with Pearl on her lap, smiling. Mother and Saoirse, improbably holding hands. Jim Gildea smiling apologetically from the doorway. How on earth had she captured that? Moll and Ellen walking side by side along the edge of a stream in the Shannon callaghs. Pearl sitting up in her buggy, pointing straight at the camera and laughing. Josh, with his hand over his beautiful face, turning away from the shot, moving behind the trunk of a tree. And Saoirse, smiling, happy in her world.

SUCCESSION

Mother came home from work upset.

Richard had called to see her. The name spun uselessly for a moment in Saoirse's head before attaching itself to the image of her dark-eyed uncle, who'd called Mother a whore and told them to leave the funeral. Mother was whispering to Nana in the kitchen but her whispers always travelled through the house from room to room through the walls and doors. She was telling Nana that he'd marched in like he owned the place, wearing a suit. He must have come straight from his office in Limerick. Saoirse wondered what her uncle did in his office. Something secret, she thought, or secretive at least; she imagined him standing at a bank of screens, behind a row of seated operatives, with his arms folded and a finger to his mouth in pensive consideration of the movements of people on the streets and along roads, giving short barked orders about who was to be allowed to go where, who was to be stopped in their tracks, who was to be arrested, who could be free.

What stupid, childish things to think. But it was a powerful image, and exciting. She'd store it away. Mother's voice was now a subdued monotone, and Nana was making sympathetic sounds. Richard had called, it seemed, to let her know that her father was ill, and it was terminal. But his mind was as sharp as ever it was. His heart is failing at last, imagine. Mother was speaking in a loving tone about her father's heart. Saoirse wondered how they'd been so strong about their grudges, how they'd managed to keep them alive for so long. What kind of wickedness was in us at all, Mother was saying to Nana now, To say we couldn't leave the past in the past? What kind of blackness came down over us? I blame my mother for it all, you know. She had him told I was never to set foot inside the door again, and that's why he let Richard run us the day of the funeral. That's why he never came afterwards to try to make it up. He could not go against her, living or dead.

The dead have a hold on us all, Nana said. And the thing about them is they'll never change their minds. Mother laughed bitterly. And she told Nana that there was a clause in her father's will stipulating that the stretch of land at the east side of their farm was to be given to her. The shallow valley that held the lake with the island at its centre where Richard and Mother had reigned their childhood summers. With watering rights reserved for the farm. So she and Richard would be drawn back together. But Richard wanted her to waive her bequest, to sign it over to him. Fuck him, Mother said. Those few fields and our puddle is the least I deserve. He won't best the Queen of Dirt Island.

DRAMA

Pearl was starting now to try to walk.

She pulled herself upwards and roared her delight at this thrilling new aspect, her new view of the world, her new power over gravity, before whumping back onto her bottom with a sweet *oof.* She pointed from the buggy and screeched at birds and dogs and passers-by, at clouds and trees and the small waves that lapped the foreshore where they sat, Saoirse and Honey and sometimes Josh, and Pearl rolling and crawling and trying to make herself mobile enough to get to the sparkling water, to rebaptize herself in its silty shallows.

Saoirse wondered how Honey could bear these expanses of space and time, having lived her life in a city, where millions of people moved around each other, colliding and living and dying in the same small spaces. There was a market outside her window where traders hollered from the early morning and you could buy anything that you wanted. You could buy a human there, if you had the money, Honey said. Saoirse felt a thrill at the thought of this, and a fear: she imagined Pearl in such a place, where all sorts of terrors and excitements waited outside her door, love and sex and heartbreak and joy, all the dramas of the world.

Honey said she'd had a life of drama. She never wanted to be involved in drama again as long as she lived, she said. And she told Saoirse about her parents and their terrible love, how they couldn't survive together or apart, how they were like fuel and flame together. Her life had been full of fear, she said, for a long time. Fragmented and chaotic and ever-changing. Her mother had left her and her father and had never really come back to her. She had more children with another man, whom Honey barely knew. She told Saoirse about her father's pure heart and wounded mind, what had happened to him at a place called Goose Green, down at the bottom of the far side of the world. What the hell were they doing sending my dad there?

Saoirse wished she could be the one to have that line to say. Just as Honey had said it. In rage and sadness, in a soft, sweet voice. She wished she could have Honey's height and slender hands, her long legs and heavy braided hair. She wished the cars that slowed to a near stop as they walked the lake road were doing so for her, at the sight of her, at the shock of her unexpected beauty. She felt a strange pride and a washing tide of happiness at the sight of Honey, swinging Pearl upwards from her buggy seat into her arms, and Pearl placing a chubby hand on each of Honey's cheeks, their eyes meeting, and their lips. She understood why Honey said she wanted to make films, slow and quiet, with no drama in them, or tension, or violence, just love.

STEPS

They came finally, her first steps.

Saoirse realized that her focus had narrowed itself to this, to her daughter beginning a journey that could last a hundred years. Or more: who knew what breakthroughs might be made in medicine or science? There might someday be a cure for death. She remembered how she'd liked science at school, nearly as much as English. Maybe she should have stayed to do her exams. Fuck the nuns. They'd have had to get over it. They'd have had to live with her swollen body and her aura of sin. She'd heard stories of women being left in terrible pain during childbirth by nursing sisters who mocked them, saying, You had your pleasure, now here's your pain. Fucking jealous bitches, Mother said. Frustration, you see, at living only half a life. Married to Jesus. Some husband He was. At least He never pissed on the floor, I suppose. God forgive me.

And Sister Laelia at least would have been kind. Most of the teachers were laypeople anyway. She remembered, though, the ranking of her classes, the girls from the Pantheon who'd tortured Breedie, and how they'd chat in civics class to the teacher about some tournament at the tennis club where they were all members, condescending to the teacher, who was careful about her speech around them, making obsequious jokes about their family businesses – Now, Miss Considine will know all about *this* because her father is a *solicitor*, won't you, Miss Considine? But it was all the same now. This was life enough for the moment. Her room, a small bit crooked in the wall for all Mother's care with her plumb line. Her baby, happy, growing before her eyes. Her mother and her grandmother standing guard against the prurience and censure of the world, deflecting every question, every attempt to get to the bottom of the whys and wherefores of Pearl's existence, to solve the mystery of her provenance. A mystery Saoirse was hardly able to contend with herself. A fumble in the dark, a blurred and misremembered thing. No pleasure, anyway, except maybe in the very moment of its half-happening, in the feeling on her face of his long hair, the momentary blaze in his eyes through the dark. And then Breedie, mauled and torn, holding herself together on the wet grass beneath a tree, her father shouting at her to come on, unsurprised it seemed at her condition, or uncaring.

In the sitting room that evening Nana and Mother sat facing one another. They were picking Pearl up and placing her on her feet, shouting, Walk! Pearl, walk! And she was laughing at the game and at their excitement, trying her best to keep herself upright, to move forward through the tiny universe between their pairs of outstretched hands, and a song was playing on the television as finally she began her long walk through her life, a number-one smash hit around the world, and it was her father singing it.

PRIDE

Josh and Honey had a life beyond, of course.

How could they not? They invited Saoirse to join them when they went places, but she knew not to impose on them, that they were asking mostly out of kindness. They drove sometimes in Josh's mother's car to the beach, and once or twice they camped the whole weekend, right up on the cliffs above the ocean. Honey went sometimes to Limerick on the morning bus with Josh, and spent the day there while he worked, looking at paintings in a gallery that Saoirse hadn't known existed, and at exhibits in a museum that sounded like she'd brought it from London with her. She went to watch films, and Saoirse pictured her, sitting low in her seat, her long legs crossed and her hands placed demurely one on top of the other, the colour and the light of the movie reflected in her brown eyes. Then she'd meet Josh in the evening and they'd bus it home, alighting at the yellow bridge, walking the back-roads to the village, holding hands.

A fight broke out in a pub in Nenagh one night. Someone had started singing a song, something stupid that they'd just made up, *Oh, Honey, Honey, you make me feel so funny, you make me feel so FIIIIINE, oh, Honey, Honey*, and the singer had put one hand on Honey's hip and one on her shoulder and had danced her across the pub floor as he sang. People had been laughing and singing along, even the group of friends that Josh and Honey had been sitting with, though the singing dancer was not a friend of theirs, and was known to be a brawler, messy in drink. Honey had gone along with the joke for one turn of the sticky carpet and had put her hand up then to push herself free, and the guy had wobbled backwards. When he regained his balance he lunged forward again and Josh had stepped in from an angle and punched him on the side of the head, connecting cleanly with the hardest part of his cheekbone, knocking him to the floor. There was a melee then and the barman stepped in, ejecting Josh and Honey for their own safety, and they'd gotten a lift home with someone from the village, and Honey's anger and Josh's resentment had been simmering and bubbling ever since, and the seething, smouldering tension between them threatened to recombust at any moment into flames.

Saoirse didn't know why this pleased her. She tried to gauge some understanding of her callous pleasure at their discord but she couldn't. When they were talking about the fight to Mother and Nana and her, Honey caught Josh looking with pride at his still swollen knuckles. She screamed at him suddenly, You fucking idiot, you stupid fucking idiot, that's nothing to be proud of! And the house seemed to shake in its foundations as the front door slammed in its frame behind her.

BOOKS

They talked a lot about books.

Some of them were books she'd read. Like *The Catcher in the Rye*. Mother had a paperback copy with a grey cover and just the title and the author's name on the front and the spine broken and its glue cracked so that the yellowing pages were all coming loose. Josh declared once that he hated the book, that Holden Caulfield was a spoilt, middle-class, narcissistic know-it-all, rebelling against nothing, kicking against invisible pricks. Must have been like looking in a mirror, then, Honey said, and she laughed, and Josh laughed, too, and said, *Touché*. Saoirse knew what that meant. That Honey's comeback had been clever, incisive. She wanted to tell them what she'd thought when she'd read the book, how she'd loved the part where Holden thought about his mother buying him skates, and asking the shop assistant all sorts of questions, and still getting the wrong ones. How Holden said that thought broke his heart and how he'd seemed beautiful to her in that moment, this teenager from half a century ago who'd never really existed except as ink on paper. Holden had Josh's face now in her imagination, and Josh's faintly embarrassed air, his narrow limbs and his ungainliness, his constant blurry aura of heartbreak.

But Josh was protesting now that *he* wasn't middle class

anyway, that a boy from a family of labourers, of cottiers, of tenants, who worked on a *factory floor*, for Christ's sake, could not be considered even close to middle class, and she lost her nerve. They were using words now in their argument that Saoirse didn't quite understand, words that had surely never before been uttered on this grassy boreen between the Gladneys' cottage and the main road, and she wondered if they meant to exclude her, if some latent meanness in them intended her to feel inadequate, unread, childish. She wanted to tell them about Lorna Doone, foundling of vagabonds, and loyal John Ridd, and how she'd loved every page of that book, but she didn't know if that was the kind of book they would think was intelligent or worthy or cool. She doubted it and so she said nothing, just walked along beside them, pretending to concentrate on keeping Pearl settled, on avoiding the bumpy bits and potholes.

She remembered Sister Laelia's disdain for James Joyce. He couldn't write poetry, girls, for all his smartness. Do you know why? PLENILUNE, girls, that's why! EPITHALAMIUM! RAIMENTED! You wouldn't catch Yeats using words like those! Or lovely Austin Clarke, or even poor Kavanagh, for all his inferiority complexes! She wondered what Sister Laelia would make of Josh. She wondered what Sister Laelia would say to her, or about her, if she, Saoirse, became a writer, and had a book on the shelves of bookshops, a number-one bestseller, a book about a family of women living in a small house together and battling through their lives. But that was not her dream to dream.

DATES

Mother started to go on dates.

The word from her mouth seemed preposterous, like she was acting in a parody or a pantomime. Her too-heavy makeup and too-short skirt emphasized this preposterousness further. Nana didn't say much, just a few judicious wisecracks. Hmm. You'll have to either get a smaller arse or a bigger skirt, Eileen. Fuck off, Mother replied. Where are you going anyway? To the pictures in Nenagh and maybe for a drink in Rocky O'Sullivan's. The pictures, Nana harrumphed. You've a grand face for going to the pictures like a young one. And who is this mysterious gentleman? How is it that me and Saoirse and Pearl aren't being allowed get a look at him? What's the big secret? He's not married, is he?

No, Mary, he's not married. His wife died. Did she now? Very convenient. Convenient? Convenient that his wife died? Come on now, Mary. I don't want to fall out with you. Oh, don't worry, Nana said, drawing her cardigan tight across her bosom. Don't worry one bit. I have more to concern me now with one son in prison, one being pecked to death, and another in his grave below in Youghalarra besides worrying about you and your fancy man. Go on away and enjoy yourself and don't even look back. Myself and my girls will be fine here. Won't we, girls? DATE! shouted Pearl suddenly. DATE! DATE! DATE! GRANNY GOING DATE!

They watched through the sitting-room window as a man pulled up at the kerb and got out to open Mother's door for her. A tall man, in his mid-fifties, maybe, a good bit older than Mother. Square-jawed and silver-streaked and debonair in the quiet, unassuming way of country men with money; he wore his trousers and jacket with just the right amount of collar and cuff. He looked safe and respectable and good-natured. Nana sniffed in semi-approval, then took to the couch and drew Pearl onto her lap and sang to her, and Pearl curled into her great-grandmother and listened gravely to the sad song about a captured rebel and a wife on the eve of her widowhood.

It ended as suddenly as it had begun. Mother came home from a date with the sun not even set, and she slammed the car door behind her, and the man spun his wheels as he drove away, revving his engine angrily. Saoirse heard her saying to Nana, I didn't think he'd be a sulk. I just didn't think he'd be like that. And Nana came back then to the best of herself, and she put her hand on her daughter-in-law's hand, on the hand of her dearest friend, the woman with whom she shared her life, and she said, Eileen, my love, they're *all* sucky-babbies. You have to give them what they want or they'll kick and scream. You just have to give it to them on your own terms, bit by bit. And they laughed, those lovely women, they laughed.

NOVEL

Josh was writing a novel.

In Josh's mother's car on the way to Limerick on a rainy Saturday, he talked and talked to Honey about a man called Billy. They were on the outskirts of the city before Saoirse realized that Billy wasn't real, that Josh had made him up. Without Pearl to focus on and hold before her she was disarmed and unsure of herself; she felt a mounting obligation to add something to the conversation, to say something meaningful, or funny, or insightful, to encourage Josh in some way, to prove to the shining people in front of her that she was just as wise as them. Anything she said sounded tinny and small in her ears, even though Honey turned herself right around each time Saoirse spoke, and smiled at her, a brilliant, heartfelt smile, as though Saoirse's words delighted her, and she'd nod and say to Josh, You see? Saoirse thinks Billy is a good idea.

Josh seemed grateful for Saoirse's approval, or pretended gratitude at least. His eyes flicked to hers in the rear-view mirror and there was warmth in them, and a flash of something else, a kind of knowing humour, like he might laugh at her, but in an affectionate way, as a fond brother might laugh at a younger sister for some innocence or some endearing foible. She missed Pearl even more then. Without her child she was reduced herself to a state of childishness, buckled safely into the backseat of a car, being brought for a treat to the shopping centre by these adults, these people who slept at night in the same bed, who talked about books and writers and films that Saoirse had never heard of, who had flown in aeroplanes and lived in countries they weren't born in, had experienced things she only fantasized about, knew secrets about the world and life that she might never know.

As they walked along the concourses of the centre, looking at the fronts of shops and at the milling people pouring antlike in and out of spaces and around each other, she felt more at one with her friends, more deserving of being in their company. Honey now and then, almost, it seemed, without knowing she was doing it, put her hand on Saoirse's arm, gripping it softly as she pointed to something in a shop window or to someone who struck her as particularly comical, and when she laughed she leant in to Saoirse, and linked her arm fully, and Saoirse felt a burst of pleasure and of pride at being seen in public with people so beautiful, who were acting as if she was their equal.

In a café where they'd stopped to rest, as she returned to their table from the toilet, she saw them kissing, long and gentle. When they drew apart they looked at each other in silence for a while, smiling, and Saoirse felt inside her the dull tug of a strange new sadness.

RELEASE

There was talk of Paudie getting out again.

Nana went with Chris monthly to the prison sixty-odd miles away and always she returned with tales of her second son's various metamorphoses. He seemed to have shed his old self almost completely; he walked now always with a very straight back, and with his chin held high, and slowly, in a kind of a half-march, Nana said, where before he was forever slouched, examining the ground in front of him as he went, nearly apologizing for his own existence. And she told them how some of the men at the other tables would move their seats for him even if they weren't in his way, and people seemed to respect him and even to fear him. And he talks Irish now. Oh, he does. Irish, imagine. They couldn't get one single word of Irish into that boy's brain all the years he went to school and now he sits down above in that prison and starts spouting it out of him to myself and Chris the very same as if he was born and reared outside on one of those islands in the Atlantic and never had a word of English in his mouth. And I think he expects us to talk Irish back to him. I'll clatter him one of these days and we'll see how much fear the other yahoos have of him then. I told him, too. I said, You're not too big or too powerful a man not to be knocked off of your chair with a belt. Shut up talking Irish. Myself and Chris didn't drive all this way to listen to your mumbo jumbo.

But Nana meant none of that. She was proud of Paudie's advancement, his new sureness and authority. She enjoyed the fact that he was feared, or at least that people were wary of upsetting her for fear of falling into his disfavour. There was no knowing the reach of the organization to which Paudie had sworn himself, which he had served, it seemed, with courage and distinction, which had placed in him their trust, which had straightened his back and raised his chin and imbued him with an aura of sacredness and inviolability, and she prayed for him daily with fervour, her eyes closed tight in contemplation of all the sorrowful mysteries of life and death and all the multitudes in between, the hardships and struggles and occasional joys, that he might be freed and that he might live happily.

But God didn't hear her, or if He did He disregarded her implorations. On a wet, blustery day in April, Jim Gildea parked his squad car outside the house and walked solemnly in the yard and stood in the kitchen in his uniform, eyes downcast, his hat in his hand, and he told Mary Aylward that her son Paudie was gone, that he'd been found in his cell in the Midlands Prison, having died in the night in his sleep.

RESPECTS

For all the talk she'd heard of death, Saoirse knew little of its truth.

The thought of Paudie's rotund body, the slabs of flesh along his arms and legs and barrel chest, his thick fingers and hard palms, being lifeless now, and spiritless, was unbearable. His face in death seemed serene but unreal, a waxy approximation of her uncle, his mouth drawn upwards at its edges into a thin parody of a smile; an attempt, she supposed, to impose on his deadness an illusion of peace, of having passed happily into infinity, having been reunited with his beloved dead. He reposed in the good room of the farmhouse; the entrance hall was split along its length with a velvet rope so that comers and leavers were separated. The line of mourners stretched the length of the boreen to the main road. Chris, his poor heart smashed, held himself manfully at his brother's head, alongside his mother. Nana's mouth and eyes seemed hard and set in an aspect of defiance, of rigid insistence on dignity. The next day Paudie was orated by strangers at altar and graveside. The man the orators described was a stranger to Saoirse. She wanted to shout at the gathered people to remember his hands, how big they were, how strong, how he'd picked her up with them and held her above his head, and swung her around, and always called her *the baby*, even after she had a baby of her own.

A company of men in black berets and sunglasses, their mouths and noses covered with scarves, marched double file behind Paudie's coffin as it was shouldered through the iron gates of Youghalarra graveyard towards his family's well-stocked plot. One of them shouted orders in Irish and they saluted as Paudie was lowered beneath a tricolour into the darkness. Father Cotter paused his prayers of committal for them but otherwise acted as though they weren't there. Chris made a strange noise as the wood of the coffin met the clay of the grave, shocking in its suddenness and alienness, a long agonized cry, a heart-rending skirl of grief.

Mother's brother, Richard, was standing by the gates as they were leaving. His eyes were deep and startlingly blue in a sudden burst of watery sunlight. She remembered them as dark, almost black. He held his two hands out to Mother and she took them. She smiled at him as she asked in a low voice, What the fuck are you doing here? He smiled back and said that he was paying his respects. You're not getting that land back, Mother said, her lips almost touching his ear.

And Richard laughed softly, and he put a hand on Mother's cheek, and she put her hand on top of his. A sweet breeze blew strong and clean up from the lake as the earth above Paudie's grave was fashioned by the spades of good neighbours into a tidy mound and blanketed in wreaths of green and white.

TIDES

There's nothing anyone can do to stop the tide, but the tide will always turn itself.

Nana thinned and soured a little for a while, and retreated into rituals of intercessional novenas and daily masses. Mother and Saoirse watched her closely for fear that she'd fall ill again, but she held fast to her robustness, for all her depletion of spirit, and she rallied, and with the weeks and months she gradually reassumed her place at the head of the small household of Aylward women, and started again to take an interest in the lives of the people who passed in and out of her warm orbit.

Honey graduated from occasional waitressing to tutoring in the art college on a film studies course, and so she went three days a week on the bus with Josh to Limerick, and only called the odd day for a walk with Saoirse and Pearl, or to sit with them in the kitchen or sitting room, listening rapt to Nana as she held court. When they walked the lake road now Honey seemed often to be distracted, always thinking about something that was in the distance, some complex abstraction, important but remote, unknowable to Saoirse.

She told Saoirse about the book that Josh was writing, how he was a really good writer but that the book itself was insane. Insane? Yes, it's fucking weird and dark, and he can't seem to free himself from it. It's finished but he keeps picking at it, changing tiny things and then changing them back, Honey said. And when he gives me parts of it to read he sits and watches my face, waiting for some expression that I don't even know I make, and he starts shouting then that I hate it, that I hate his book, that I hate him. I don't know what I'm going to do, Saoirse. He's just so unhappy. How do I make him happy again?

But Saoirse didn't know. Happiness was a strange notion, something that was wrapped neatly and packed into the closing scenes of television shows and daytime films, sharply relieved on the screen but blurry in real life, a vague ideal. She wanted Pearl to be happy, of course, in a pure and uncomplicated way, and she thought that she was. She rarely cried and she laughed a lot, and she ruled her little queendom with a kind of replete joy. Joshua Elmwood's heart seemed like an unfathomably intricate concept in comparison to her daughter's, a thing impossible to conceive of or to begin to understand.

I have to leave him for a while, Honey said. And I want you to mind him for me, Saoirse. His mother and his granny love him dearly but they don't really know him like we do. Will you take care of him, please? Saoirse nodded. And Honey Bartlett bent down to kiss Pearl's head, and they continued downhill, as a murmuration of starlings swirled and dived above the placid lake.

BURSTING

The question of how exactly Saoirse was supposed to mind Josh was never properly addressed.

Honey called down to take her tearful leave on a rainy Tuesday morning and they didn't hear from Josh for weeks afterwards. When eventually he visited he was in the company of his grandmother, and they were only passing on the way to the holy well to replenish Kit's stock of blessed water. He was quiet on that visit, but he sat on the floor with Pearl, building a house with her from Lego blocks, listening carefully to her instructions. Pearl cried as he and Kit were leaving, saying that Josh hadn't finished the house, so he returned from the door and knelt again beside her, and when he'd finished the job to Pearl's satisfaction she said, Thank you, Dosh, you may go now, and they all laughed at her mispronunciation, her sweet, unaffected bossiness.

Saoirse considered walking herself up from the village to Knockagowny Hill where the Gladneys lived, as she often had before, but only ever in the company of Josh and Honey, or to call on them for an arranged meeting, to go to town together or to watch a video or to sit with them in the long annexe at the back of the cottage, built somewhere in the hazy past by Paddy Gladney and his son-in-law and great friend, Alexander, where Josh sometimes painted on an easel, and there was a low desk covered with books and pieces of paper, and there was a bed, which Honey and Josh obviously shared, that was always tossed and that had, on the floor beside it, a perpetually overflowing ashtray. The sight of the ashtray always thrilled her, and she wasn't sure why. The filmic decadence of it, maybe, the idea of a scene where Josh and Honey were naked in the moonlight, lying sheened and sheetless after making love, sharing a cigarette. She couldn't imagine herself in such a scene. As much as she'd learnt about life and death and all the blind corners in between she still didn't know what it was to lie in a bed all night with someone she loved, or to be unabashedly naked in someone's company, or how it might feel to make actual love.

Care for him, Honey had said as she was leaving. Maybe to care then would actually be enough. Maybe she wouldn't have to be active about it, but could just resign herself to intermittent visits while she gave a portion of her consciousness to a consideration of him, how he might be, whether he might be lonely without his love, who was working somewhere in the north of England on a documentary, apparently, and would be for the rest of the spring and all of the summer.

And as Saoirse was thinking these thoughts, some stressed vessel ruptured inside her grandmother as she napped on her armchair across the room, and began a slow, destructive haemorrhage in her dear head.

CARING

Isn't it a blessing that this room gets so much light? I'd hate to be in a dark room, said Nana. The hospital inside in Limerick was very dark, and they had me pushed into a corner beside a big pillar so I couldn't see window or door. And the one alongside me was in an awful way, roaring out of her every time a doctor or nurse looked at her. I said to her one day, There's nothing wrong with you if you can roar that loudly. Oh, she took terrible umbrage. I don't like them poking me, says she, and sticking me with needles every chance they get. You've a right to go on away home, so, says I to her, besides tormenting those of us who take no exception to being cured. I woke up one morning and she was gone. To earthly or to heavenly home, I don't know, nor did I ask.

Nana told the same stories over and over again. Mother would tell her to shut up sometimes, and tell her that she'd have a stroke herself if she had to hear the same fucking story twenty times a day, and Nana would take offence, lifting her chin defiantly and raising the volume on the television until Mother would stomp in and turn it down again, accusing Nana of being deaf as well as crippled. Imagine talking to me like that, Nana would say. But Saoirse couldn't imagine Mother *not* talking to Nana like that, and she was glad of Mother's unwaveringly impolitic nature, her peculiar loving manner, and she knew that Nana loved Mother with the same gruff constancy.

Nana's left side had been struck. Half of me is gone, she said, and the other half is following hard behind. But she still had some movement in her left arm and leg, and she might even walk again, her doctor said. A physiotherapist called twice a week, a plain girl with a refined accent and hands that Nana said were stronger than you'd think for such a slip of a one, but always very cold. She manipulated Nana's arm and leg and left instructions for daily exercises, to be undertaken with the help of Saoirse or Mother, or even Doreen or Chris, who called often and seemed happy in each other's company, although still no sign of chick nor child.

Josh took to calling in the evenings after work. As the summer days stretched themselves towards their equinox he became a daily visitor to the side of Mary Aylward's high mechanized bed, in the middle of the sitting room of her daughter-in-law's house, and he'd sit with her and Saoirse in comfortable silence reading, or chatting about his day, the factory floor and all its petty machinations, and Nana, buoyed by their captive attentions, would tell them about her life and all the people in it, the living and the dead, and all the things she'd do if she were young again.

IGNORING

Josh without Honey was less talkative, seemed less confident.
Or maybe he just didn't think that Saoirse was very interesting, or worthy of the effort of animated words. She watched
as he told Nana news from the village, carried second-hand
from his mother and grandmother. Mother would pass in and
out and sometimes Saoirse would hear her laugh or exclaim
softly from the kitchen. Saoirse counted the number of times
Josh would look at her while he spoke. Sometimes the number
was zero. As if she wasn't there.

In the mornings and early afternoons when Mother was at
work Saoirse and Pearl gave Nana all of their attention. Pearl
took to climbing onto the high bed and sitting primly against
its baseboard, making villages of teddies and dolls, and involv-
ing Nana in their societies. Nana was a good patient, asking
for nothing more than a cup of tea and a slice of toast, and now
and again, a grilled rasher. When I'm back on my feet we're
going to go somewhere, she said one day. All of us women.
We'll go out west and stay in a hotel by the sea. Won't that be
fun? Lord, it will. I'm looking forward now to standing with
my poor feet in the ocean. There's great healing in saltwater,
you know. Sometimes in the evenings Mother and Saoirse
would lower the bed and transfer Nana into her wheelchair, on
loan, like her bed, from the Midwestern Health Board, and

wheel her to the bathroom where between them they'd draw her onto her good leg, and Saoirse would support her with all of her strength while Mother quickly disrobed her, and then they'd sit her on the edge of the bath, and swing her a half-circle around, and down into her bath seat in the water. It was important to get the temperature right. Mother often spent more than twenty minutes running taps and cursing and accusing her temperature gauge of being faulty before committing Nana to the bathwater, and when Nana complained that the water was too cold or too hot Mother would tell her it was the exact right temperature, the same exact temperature as it always was, and to shut her face or she'd fucking drown her, and Nana would shriek with laughter, sitting in her bath seat like a white-haired liver-spotted baby, waiting for her back to be soaped.

If Josh happened to be there at bath time he'd stay in the sitting room or kitchen and play with Pearl, patiently, never condescending or even seeming to humour her; he always affected real interest in what she was saying and doing, and Pearl seemed to grow around him, to expand her efforts at language, to speak more clearly and in longer sentences. And sometimes Saoirse would leave her mother and her grandmother in the bathroom, squabbling and splashing and threatening each other, and she'd sit and watch Josh, wondering what he was thinking, and why he was even there.

STUCK

Finally the truth was spoken, or some glib version of it.

How much truth about the invisible, silent, inner workings of a person could be contained in a single sentence? The sentence was: That boy is stuck on you. It was spoken by Nana. Saoirse ignored her, but Nana pressed on. Do you even realize it, Saoirse? That boy is stuck on you. Saoirse pretended not to know what or to whom Nana was referring. She carried on tidying the cushions from the sitting-room floor and arranging Nana's newspapers and magazines in a tidy pile on her bed stand. She said it again, louder. Saoirse! That boy is stuck on you.

Nana, what kind of rubbish are you talking? Even as she said the words some soft glimmer of the truth of Nana's assertions worked its way into the gloom of Saoirse's imagination. She saw Josh again in his calm distractions, reading stories from the paper to Nana, listening to Nana's own stories with a sweet, patient smile, sweeping his long fringe back from his brown eyes, revealing in them a depth of distant sadness. These thoughts made Saoirse's stomach burn, caused a tingling at the ends of her fingers and toes, as though her heart had in the moment of revelation and epiphany forgotten itself and shuddered and stopped in shock, before resuming its steady beat.

He has a bad case, God help us. And why wouldn't he?

You're a pure solid picture, so you are, and you're a great girl, and you're a great little mother. And in this day and age it's no impediment to romance, having children for different fellas. NANA! SHUT UP! I will not shut up. It's painful watching ye, ignoring one another. Why do ye think he's here every second evening? Do you think 'tis my dusty bones are drawing him in that door and only half of me working and I as old as Ireland? I am in my tail. The other lady fecked off on him without so much as a by your leave and so has no claim on him as far as I'm concerned. Your grandfather was doing a strong line with a one from Templederry when we started courting, you know. He dallied the two of us for a good while until we all ended up at the one dance below in the Golden Vale Ballroom and her brothers were there and they gave him a right good dusting and that was that.

So go on, granddaughter, Nana said. Strike in the name of God while the iron is hot, let you. Stop, Nana. There's no way I'd do that to Honey. And, anyway, you're wrong. He doesn't care about me, at least not as more than a friend.

Ah, friend, my arse, Nana said, and she seemed now to be properly cross. You only get one life, and no woman should spend any part of it being friends with men. That's not what men are for.

MOVE

What could be done?

Saoirse took a doleful stock of herself. Twenty-one years of age with a three-year-old daughter. No Leaving Certificate, never even had a job. Never really had a proper boyfriend, except Oisín who'd hardly been more than a crush that grew into an obsession in her mid-teens and ended in a burst of anger in an alleyway in Nenagh. Her greatest joy in life, besides her daughter, whose unlikely father didn't know she was alive, and outside of the narrow confines of the bungalow she lived in with her mother and her grandmother in a small estate in a village that nobody'd ever heard of, tucked between a hillside and a lake, was a friendship that seemed now to have ended with a girl from London whom she'd loved and, almost completely unknown to herself, been jealous of, in equal measure.

If the truth of Nana's words were to be acted on, it would have to be by Josh. There was no way she could make a move. How could that possibly even work? Would she sneak up on him some evening as Nana dozed and plant her lips on his? Or whisper to him, Will we go for a walk? And take his hand then while they walked and see if he drew his hand away? She imagined herself doing crazy things like biting his ear suddenly as he sat beside her on the couch, or plunging her fingers down the back of his jeans and pulling him backwards onto the ground and straddling him, her knees pinning his arms, slapping him in his face over and over again until his cheeks were bright red, his wide, shocked eyes full of tears. Love me, not her, love *me*!

It had been six weeks. Honey hadn't written. She had the number of Saoirse's new mobile but she hadn't rung or sent a text as she'd said she would. Josh hadn't mentioned anything to Saoirse about how she'd been getting on, and whenever Nana asked after her he said she was fine, she was getting on well, but his words seemed flat and hollow, rote, spoken automatically and containing no real information. He'd redden a little at the tops of his ears and high on his cheeks, like someone who was lying, or embarrassed. Whenever this happened Nana would wink over at Saoirse and raise her eyebrows while nodding towards Josh. He definitely saw her doing it a few times, but he pretended not to notice.

Saoirse wanted Josh. Badly she wanted him. Her memories of Honey now were scored and soured, their pristineness sullied, their innocence made degenerate by her desire for Josh, to press her face against his naked chest and feel his dear heart beating there, to put her hands either side of his beautiful, sad face and press her lips against his lips, to sweep his hair back from his eyes and say, I love you, and to hear him say it back.

AFFAIR

Is that what you'd call it?

Josh said the word suggested illicitness and transgression. But their thing was neither of those. Thing? You know what I mean, our . . . our . . . and he couldn't seem to find a word that would explain their walks through the callaghs, following a path by the shallow stream that led from the village to the shore of the lake, and stopping there on a tiny half-moon of shingle beach, sitting together on a low wide branch of a smoothly barked tree, putting their arms around each other and kissing, sometimes hard and sometimes soft, clashing teeth and tongues, getting better at kissing each other as the evenings went by, each adapting to the other's shapes and habits.

How funny it was that it had taken him so long even to kiss her. The first evening they'd walked alone together, at Nana's behest, it had been obvious to them both that it would happen. Something fizzed and crackled in the air between them, some excitement of the atoms in their shared atmosphere and on their skin; it was damply hot as they walked together, and there were great spaces of silence between them, broken by Saoirse's observation that Nana was gas, and Josh's response that she was a ticket all right, and that he was very fond of her, and that he loved calling in to them, that it broke the monotony of the factory and the cottage, that he loved his mother and granny but they had their fixed routines that he had to try to fit into, or not get in the way of, and Saoirse nearly asked him about Honey, how they could be about to do what they both knew they were about to do to her, but they didn't do anything that first evening, or the next evening; three times they walked along the stream's raised bank above the heavy tangle of summer growth and down to their tree by the water, hidden from the world, before finally, shyly, hesitantly, like a boy who'd never been anywhere or done anything or slept for countless nights beside a girl as beautiful as Honey, he picked up her hand and held it in his and said her name, just once, and when she turned her face to his he kissed her.

And one evening at the end of their first fortnight Josh drew her downwards from the branch, onto the soft damp ground at the water's edge, and they were nearly naked and the sky above them was a cold still blue and Josh's eyes were closed above her, and she wondered why he wasn't looking at her, and she was about to tell him to stop when he opened his eyes, and she saw in them a light reflected from her own eyes, and she chose to believe that it was love that she saw there, furiously lit, and she drew him down and into her, and it was love, it was.

NOTEBOOKS

S he wondered about his life with Honey.

Had she a right to know? He hardly ever mentioned her. When he did he'd cast his eyes downwards, in shame, she presumed, or in embarrassment at his behaviour. She wanted badly to know exactly what he was thinking but she was afraid to ask him. She wanted to be worldly and sophisticated like Honey, to just know things, to pick up reflexively, effortlessly on the cues and signals that people emitted, to read the truth of them through the gaps between their words and actions. Was he embarrassed of her? To be seen walking the roads with her, or driving with her in his mother's car? She was younger than him, but only a few years. Maybe Pearl was an issue, much as he seemed to love her. He asked once who the father was, and when she told him he laughed and said, Yeah, right. She didn't try to make him believe her and he didn't ask again. Pearl's father was very famous now, but whenever she thought about him or heard him on the radio or saw him with his band on TV, her feelings amounted to no more than a blurry impression of his shape in the darkness, and of his hair tickling her face as she lay beneath him.

Mother knew what was going on, and Nana of course knew: it was all Nana's idea in a way. But now that her idea was realized she was silent about the romance. Saoirse had expected conspiratorial conversations, winks and elbows, knowing smiles. But Nana adopted a strangely aloof aspect when Josh visited now, and a vague weight of awkwardness permeated the air. Still he called and sat patiently on the floor with Pearl, arranging her little worlds with her, or on the armchair by Nana's bed, and he even pushed Nana in her wheelchair, a taste of the way down the lake road, as she put it. Just a taste, young Elmwood. Don't bring me too far or you'll never get me back. And after a little while the air between them lightened, thinned again. Honey faded to an abstraction, a dim, distant frisson of guilt, easily ignored.

Josh showed Saoirse a pile of A4 notebooks one late summer evening in a corner of the room in his grandparents' cottage that he used to share with Honey. They were stacked neatly and their covers had been laminated, and on each cover was a wide white sticker, on which was written a concise summary of the contents of the timeworn pads. NOTES. POEMS. STORIES. BILLY SHEARS BOOK 1. BILLY SHEARS BOOK 2. BILLY SHEARS BOOK 3. She asked him who Billy Shears was. He was silent for a long time. She wondered if he'd heard her. Eventually he pushed his hair back from his face, and said, Me. Billy Shears is me. And she realized then that he was crying, but she knew no way to ask him why.

DEVIL

He said weird things sometimes.

Like that he often felt the presence of the devil around him. She knew that he was saying that to see how she'd react. They were lying naked under a thin blanket in his bed. His mother and his grandmother were in the city; Pearl was safe with Mother and Nana. They'd had hours together, and it had been all so lovely, and exciting, and then relaxed and comfortable afterwards, and she could see why people talked so much about sex, obsessed about it, wrote books and made films about it and killed each other over it and made it the subject of all kinds of art. It was so beautiful when the person you did it with was a person you loved and trusted, and who wanted to please you, and to whom you felt so attracted that the thought of them, the idea of them, the memory of their touch, was enough to light you from inside in the dead of night and fill you with a warmth that spread from the top of your head to the very tips of your toes.

And then these small unexpected proclamations could intrude so easily and make little scratches and rips in her happiness, working at it until it started to tear and bleed. These sudden weird whispers about the devil or darkness or life being filled with pain. Why would he say that to her? Lying here, with her head resting on his bare chest, in silence, while he slowly smoked a cigarette, blowing thin bluish lines towards the ceiling, it seemed as though he'd felt obliged to say something unexpected and bizarre, something that would chime with some idea he had of himself, or an idea he wanted her to have of him. Of someone dark, intense, complex. But she saw him as handsome and kind, a little bit unsure of himself, and sometimes, in certain situations, endearingly arrogant, like a child convinced they're good at something that they've just started to do.

He stubbed his cigarette and read to her from one of his Billy Shears notebooks. It sounded at first like a really old-fashioned poem and it changed then into a story about a man waking up and not knowing where he was or who he was and he was being nursed by some kind of phantom figures who fed him and gave him some sweet narcotic drink that kept him in their thrall, and he acted out all the parts in a booming voice, or a weak croak, or a harsh whisper, and he stopped reading suddenly, and he looked at her closely, and he said, The devil whispered all that to me. Into my ear he whispered it. He asked her if that scared her, and she nodded. And she knew that he was glad that she was scared. And this knowledge pressed against her heart, causing her an abject sorrow of a kind she'd never felt before.

FALLING

B ut still, he was mostly beautiful, and always gentle.
Even when he was saying strange things and reading to
her from the novel that Honey had told her was insane. And
what would Honey know about it? She was a different kind of
artist from Josh: she seemed obsessed with capturing something about people from the way they posed themselves and
the way they spoke: she'd spent whole days making Josh introduce her to the oddest of people around the parish, and she'd
made recordings of them speaking about themselves on her
little camera. People like Mickey Briars, who was a builder and
lived on his own in a tiny thatched cottage on the lake road,
right at the entrance to the callaghs, whose mother everyone
said used to be a witch, and who used to solve all sorts of prob-
lems for women and girls. Or Bridget Toppy, who was a
Traveller, and lived in a tiny house with a wagon wheel bolted
to its gable wall.

She felt herself falling deeper and deeper. From her first
waking moments she thought about him. Mam, Mam, Mam,
Pearl would shout, her voice rising and rising as she tried to
gain purchase on her mother's awareness, tried to insinuate her
way back into the place she had occupied effortlessly since her
first moment of life, the centre of her mother's attention. But
Saoirse was often absent now, distracted, watching out the

window hours before he was due to appear at the entrance to the estate, swinging the gear bag that he took to work in his left hand, carrying some small gift for her or for Nana in his other hand, a bottle of wine or a box of chocolates or a book. For the love of God, Nana said one day, will you snap out of it, girl? If I'd known you'd lose your mind like this I'd never have egged you on the way I did.

A long letter arrived from Honey. She was in Scotland, on an island off the highland coast, making a new film about women who farmed the harsh land alone. Her letter was full of details about the people she was working with and the women whose lives they were documenting, but she made no mention of when she'd be finished, or of coming back. Saoirse imagined a day somewhere in the dim future when a letter would arrive and Honey would say, It's okay. I know all about you and Josh. I wanted it to happen. I love you both. Give my love to my goddaughter. Goodbye. And Honey then could be apotheosized into a kind of a patron saint of their love, or a guardian angel, a beautiful celestial light of creation, omniscient and loving and sublime.

But a hard, wise part of her believed that would never happen. As happy as she was in her first headlong rush into love, part of her felt already the bitter pangs of inevitable pain.

HEAVEN

Who are we like?

Dylan Thomas and Vera Phillips? F. Scott Fitzgerald and Zelda? Yeats and Georgie Hyde-Lees? We're like none of those, she said. All of those people are dead. And those women all sound like they have horsy faces. She caught herself hoping that he'd enter this opening she'd made and say something about her face, something that would hint at least at what he thought about how she looked. Or even maybe put his hand on her cheek and caress it and kiss it and say, You look nothing like any of them. She wanted him to say she was beautiful, and the depth of her wanting made her feel sick. But he was in his act again: he'd stepped out of himself and into the skin of aloof pretension he seemed to assume after sex. He was lying at an angle from her, one hand behind his head, smoking. Maybe we are both dead, he said. Maybe we're dead and this is Hell.

She stood and picked up her shoes from the floor. She threw one of them at him, hard, and hit him in his chest. He looked stung for a moment but otherwise he didn't react. This Saturday had started so well, with him calling early and asking her if she wanted to take a walk to the lake, and they had, and they'd brought Pearl, and she'd walked most of the way holding his hand and talking sweet nonsense nonstop. Then they'd spent the afternoon lazing in a bath of sunlight around Nana's daybed, talking in fits and starts, listening to Nana's barely believable stories about people she knew who came from families of more than twenty children, of women giving birth in the morning and milking cows in the evening, or miscarrying as they walked to the river for water and cleaning themselves in the river and going home and saying no more about it. Oh, yes. There was no ollagoaning in them days.

Hell. Why couldn't he have said Heaven? He said he'd meant Hell as in life is hell, life is composed of suffering. Oh, for fuck's sake, she said. Suffering? All you do is get the bus to Limerick and glue bits of plastic together and call down to me for a ride whenever you feel like it. What suffering? He smoked on, maddeningly, not looking at her, moving his hand in an exaggerated arc through the stale bedroom air up to and away from his lips. His other arm was behind his head, his elbow crooked upwards; her words seemed to have no effect on him. You put on a great act of being nice, she said. You're fake.

His eyes then had hurt in them, and she softened. She climbed back onto his bed and curled into him. They lay silently together in the dull winter light. After a while he whispered, This is Heaven, and she closed her eyes against a sudden well of tears.

PEEPING

Doreen rang her mobile one evening near Christmas. Her voice sounded strange, low and hoarse, and she was speaking slowly and carefully, like someone not used to speaking on a phone. She asked Saoirse to call up to her the next day if she could, for a visit just, that Chris had mentioned that he hadn't seen his niece or his grandniece in a good long while and he was anxious to say hello to them. Don't tell your mother that you're calling, Doreen said. She'll only be feeling obliged to send up tarts and I have enough of tarts made here to feed an army. I have tarts up the wazoo, Doreen said, and her voice crackled suddenly into a strange unexpected laughter, high and thin, a kind of manic ululation. Saoirse couldn't remember ever having heard her laugh before. She promised to call the next day at lunchtime.

Doreen was waiting at the farmhouse door. Pearl regarded her balefully. Inside at the ancient oak table that had served countless Aylwards and was still stout and solid on its legs they sat, Saoirse facing Doreen, and Pearl playing by the parlour door with Chris's ageing collie, which basked in joy at her touch, her unadulterated love. Now, lady, Doreen said suddenly. I have you here at last. There was a strange didactic harshness in her voice that ignited a flame across Saoirse's middle. There'd been no offer of tea, no sign of anything at all having been prepared, not even a tart for all her talk, though she'd stipulated they were to call at lunchtime. There was no sign of Chris and the kitchen felt bare and sterile, stringently cleaned.

I saw you, Doreen said. Her words crossed the space between them like a sudden slap. I saw you. With the boy of the Elmwoods. Below in the callaghs. There was a catch in her voice, a hitching of breath as though she were nervous, or was being overwhelmed by emotion. Saoirse's stomach burned again, and she felt a sudden need to go to the toilet. I saw you, she said again. Ye didn't think anyone could see what ye were doing. You leaning against the trunk of a tree and young Elmwood behind you and your skirt up around your waist and your knickers down and he going at you like a young bull. And that poor child asleep in her buggy at the edge of the water. Some mother you are, lady. She could have been drowned while you were being . . . being . . . *serviced*. The child could have been *drowned*.

Doreen was gripping the table edge now, and she was leaning towards Saoirse. Her face was a violent shade of red and her eyes were dark with hate. You don't deserve to have that child. Look at her. Look at her. How innocent she is. What kind of world is this at all? To say you'd be given a child like that and I given nothing. Nothing.

SORRY

Tears then.

Saoirse now was in a place she'd never been before. She hardly knew Doreen. She was shocked by the picture of herself that Doreen presented. That had happened only once, a kiss against their secret tree that had spilt like a storm surge over a breakwater into a frantic splash, and she'd felt equal parts thrilled pleasure and abject fear, but Pearl had been asleep, and her stroller had been facing away from them, and there had seemed no way to stop it, no way to push back against the torrent. She hadn't known they could be seen in their tiny clearing on the dense foreshore: there was no path to their spot, no way of knowing about it. Doreen must have been somewhere on the banked earth that ran along the side of the stream that entered the lake beside their tiny beach, watching through a tangle of briars and branches.

Even in this rank stew of mortification and shame she felt deep within herself a distant hum of excitement as the memory of the pleasure of it rose unbidden, the scorching heat of desire and the incredible, rapturous surge, the wave of climax building and breaking across her whole body. The idea of Doreen watching them ignited some strange new intensity, and she pushed it away, repulsed and amazed at her own imposturous impulses.

I didn't mean to say that to you. I didn't mean to. I only meant to ask you would you call up more often, and would you bring the child with you. Chris would kill me if he knew I talked to you like that. He won't hear a bad word spoken about you or your mother or his own mother. I don't know why I spoke like that to you. I think sometimes I'm losing my mind. She sobbed then, loud, almost shrieking with pain. It's none of my business what you do. Saoirse considered taking Doreen's hand in hers, but something about the sight of the thin bones pressing out against her mottled skin, the thought that her skin would be as cold as the marbled skin of Paudie's dead face, stopped her.

Ye're all so taken with one another. Mary and Eileen and you. I'm the exact relation to Mary that your mother is, you know. I'm more of a relation, actually, because I'm married to her only living son. Your mother could go off and remarry any time. I'm living here in her house doing my damnedest to be a wife to her son and she barely gives me the time of day. I'm a show opposite my own family and all the neighbours over the way she went down to live with ye. Ye're all wrapped up together in one bundle below in that housing estate and I'm left up here stranded.

I have no one, I have no one, Saoirse, no one in the world to love and no one in the world loves me.

PLEA

Surely Chris loved her.

Why otherwise would he have married her? He came in from the fields, as gangly and blue-eyed as ever, thinner maybe, more lined around his eyes in the months since the short miles of distance between them had last been closed. Doreen suddenly was full of movement and talk, explaining to Chris that she had no tea wet and not even a sandwich made because they'd been chatting like mad, hadn't we, Saoirse, and Saoirse smiled and said they had, and Chris seemed delighted at this new camaraderie, this new consideration by his niece for his lonesome wife, and he picked Pearl up and swung her around and covered her chubby face with kisses while Doreen stood at the worktop making lunch, her elbows working furiously up and down, her butter-knife smacking rhythmically against the thick sliced bread.

Later Doreen walked the boreen to the road with them, holding Pearl's hand. In the mesh basket under the seat of Pearl's stroller was a fruitcake wrapped in greaseproof paper. Mary loves my fruitcake, Doreen said. It's the one thing about me she likes! And she laughed her reedy laugh again, and Saoirse could find no placatory words so she laughed as well, and heard herself saying, Ah, now, appropriating Doreen's own locutions. Doreen said then, in a low voice, I wasn't spying, you know. I was doing the route I always do from here to Bally-rusheen to the callaghs and back up the lake road. I just happened to be passing the one gap where you can see in to that spot just at the time that ye were . . . I shouldn't even have looked. I should have walked on. Anyway, how's ever. I'll never tell anyone what I saw, that I promise. She stopped and straightened herself to her full height, just shy of Saoirse's five feet six. Her thin nostrils flared, and Saoirse could see a skim of grease on the skin of her face, a wild bloom of opened pores along her nose and cheeks. Her grey-green eyes bulged a little against the skin of their sockets.

Will you please come back up soon? I'll never again talk to you the way I did today. We'll be down at Christmas, but will you come up here as well? There was a new tremor in her voice now. I can mind Pearl any time, you know. I'm here on my own all the day long. Would you leave her with me once in a wonder, even? I'm not mad. I swear to you, I'm not mad. You can go about your business and she'd be happy and safe here with me. I'd show her the cows and the chickens and the baby lambs. And Saoirse felt within herself a rising, flooding sad-ness, for this woman and her barren attenuated life, and with it a savage unspoken resentment at what was being implied. That Doreen would mind her daughter while she got fucked against a tree.

SITTING

Doreen started to call once or twice a week.

To sit with Nana, she said, and at the start it was an uncomfortable arrangement. Doreen would assure Saoirse that she could go and do her own thing if she wanted; Nana would shake her head and purse her lips and draw her good hand across her throat in warning to Saoirse not to leave her on her own with her odd, occluded daughter-in-law. Doreen was solicitous and deferential with Nana, but uncomfortable around her counterpart; Mother had a habit of standing over her, her feet set a little bit too far apart, her hands on her hips, looking down at her and asking questions, like, Well, Doreen, how are things on the farm? How's our Chris? Is he doing a bit of contracting? All innocuous, everyday questions, but asked with a palpable edge of aggressive derision, and it struck Saoirse that Doreen must think that she'd told Mother about Doreen's fit, her mad broadside, and that Mother was just waiting for an opening for an all-out attack. So Doreen visited mostly in the mornings when Mother was at work.

After a while Nana began to soften towards Doreen, who it seemed was possessed of an insatiable prurience and a vast store of information about all the people of the parish and surrounding townlands. She knew things that Nana could only dream of knowing, given the narrowness of her sphere of interaction. Doreen prefaced all of her pronouncements with *They say*, or *They maintain*, or *They make out*, and affected an air of impartiality and judiciousness in her delivery in order to distance herself from the salacity of the gossip-mongers and idlers from whom she garnered her stories. She'd heard it said that Mickey Briars below the road had several bodies buried in the wild acre behind his cottage and that was why he cultivated its wildness to such a degree. She had it from a man that Chris sold a dog to that two people not far at all from where they were sitting right now were involved with drugs and prostitutes. She had stories of secret gays, swinging couples, violent husbands, faithless wives, transvestites, sex rings, drug rings, covered-up murders. She stayed away from subversive activity and gunrunning or anything that might strike too close to Nana's bones.

She developed a line of patter with Pearl that was stilted and fragmentary at first, but that developed in warmth and fluency with the weeks, and Pearl began to watch out the window for Doreen and to shout in excitement when she saw her appear at the entrance to the estate, beating her small-stepped path, hunched and raincoated, to their door. And one spring day Pearl met Doreen at the door with a chain of daisies in her little hand, and she told Doreen it was a crown for her, and Doreen bent to receive her diadem, and when she straightened Saoirse saw that her eyes were full of tears.

RECONCILIATION

Mother tried twice to see her father.

Saoirse heard her from the kitchen one rainy Friday evening, telling Nana her plans. I'm going to say sorry, Mary. I'll have to. I'll have to tell him I'm sorry. And he'll say that he's sorry, too, I know well he will. Nana made some kind of placatory sound, and Mother went on, in a lower voice so that Saoirse couldn't quite make out what was being said. But she knew, and the knowledge flared inside her for a moment, burning her, before settling to a low smoulder and then extinguishing completely, that Mother's apology was about her. Mother was going to apologize to her dying father for Saoirse's existence.

So Mother went the following Sunday afternoon to her father's house. But she was met on the boreen that led through the front acres along by the island where she'd co-reigned in her childhood by Richard, coming the other way. The devil's luck it was. He wouldn't pull in to let her pass but blocked the way. He got out and stood by the door of his car and gestured to her to reverse back, but she wouldn't: she got out of her car, too, and forced him to speak. He said that there was no point in going up to the house; their father didn't want to see her and he was too weak to be getting upset. Saoirse imagined this stand-off in black and white, with Richard wearing a long coat and a trilby hat, and Mother with a headscarf and oversized sunglasses, their car doors open before them like shields against one another, cover in case their encounter blew fully into a confrontation, or a skirmish, or a gunfight. But she knew the reality of the moment, too, the spite of Richard, how the small-ness of his spirit diminished her mother's, the terrible pain of her mother's regret.

Mother went a few weeks later into Milford Hospice when an informant told her in the bookie's that her father had been taken there and that he was near his end. She came home late, but Nana and Saoirse had waited up, Nana watching the win-dow constantly, asking at the sound of every car, Is that her? Is she landed? When Mother came in from the dark night she was silent and pale. They didn't press her. After she'd settled herself she looked from Nana to Saoirse and said, I was too late. I left it too late. He didn't know me. I don't know if he could even see me.

Saoirse went to the kitchen to make tea. Through the arch-way she saw that Mother was beside Nana now, and Nana's arms were around her, hugging her tight into herself, like a mother would hug a crying child, a child who's fallen, or who's had a bad dream, who can't stop their tears from falling, as if to take from that child all their pain, and make it her own.

ORPHAN

He died a few days after Mother's fruitless visit to his bedside.

Mother came home that afternoon and addressed the news directly to Nana, as though it didn't concern Saoirse, and that was true of course, it didn't. Standing against the baseboard of Nana's daybed she said in a weirdly dreamy voice, He's gone, Mary. Last night inside in the hospice. My aunties were with him, thank God, and Richard. Oh, said Nana, blessing herself. God rest him now. And then Nana adopted a curiously formal tone, as if Mother wasn't the person closest to her in the world but an acquaintance or a distant neighbour. I'm very sorry now for your trouble, Eileen. And Mother said, Trouble is right.

Saoirse didn't know what to do or say. Mother, once the news was broken, was moving a lot, bustling from spot to spot, picking things up and tidying them away, even things that had been left out for a purpose, like Nana's *Sacred Heart Messenger* and Pearl's bucket of Lego blocks. Nana beckoned Saoirse over and whispered, She's upset, you know. She'll never let on to us but her heart is broken. He was still her father when all is said and done, and the fact that they never made up properly is killing her. It's a funny old grief she'll be feeling, God help us. And so they resigned themselves to a quiet state of loving receptiveness and acceptance of Mother's new caprices, but they never came; she held herself more or less steady and calm all that day, though there was about her a faint crackling static of nervous energy, and she left the next morning for work as usual and came home with a new navy suit and shoes from Marion's boutique on Kenyon Street, and she modelled the outfit for them and Nana declared it to be a noble rig-out and one she'd surely get plenty of wear out of. You'll have it for my funeral too, Eileen. I will, said Mother. Isn't that great? And they laughed.

Mother insisted on going alone. She avoided the house, but sat in the second row from the front at the funeral mass, she told them later, in between a brace of aunts she'd loved in childhood, and they were kind to her and she was kind to them. Her mother's family formed a blurry coterie in Saoirse's imagination, Richard's the only face with definition, standing in his black suit at the centre of the cloud of mysterious sorrow, his hair blue-black and combed back into a wavy quiff, his cheekbones sharp and high below his burning eyes. Mother came home in the late afternoon and sat in her car beneath the drizzling sky for a while before coming in. Her eyes looked weary and bloodshot; there was a smell off her of cigarettes, though she was supposed to have given up.

Now, she said, and smiled a strange, sad smile. Now the shit will hit the fan.

MANNERS

The shit hit the fan around a week later.

Saoirse and Josh had eaten supper with his mother, Moll, and his grandmother, Kit, and afterwards they'd walked across the long high meadow to the Jackmans' house, because Andrew Jackman was home from Switzerland where he lived, and he and Josh had a kind of uncomfortable but oddly sincere friendship. Andrew had been given power of attorney over his father's property and businesses and he'd gifted Josh's grandmother the caretaker's cottage she lived in and the acre of lovingly tended garden and orchard around it. Andrew had bullied Josh as a child, and Josh appeared to consider this generous act to be a kind of an apology, an acknowledgement of the hurt he'd caused, and Josh was quietly grateful for Andrew's oblique contrition, and moved by it. But he was different in Andrew's presence: he seemed to hesitate before he spoke, as if to form his words into a shape that would fit most comfortably with an idea he had of what Andrew Jackman might want to hear. He spoke about the factory where he worked in terms of markets and outputs, using esoteric words and phrases that he'd never used with Saoirse; when he mentioned the factory to her it was only ever to complain about the monotony of the work or the low pay or to tell her a story about some new fight or affair or wildness of one or other of the people who worked there.

Saoirse and Josh were sitting on a varnished loveseat beneath an arch of tangled and variegated foliage at the end of the Jackmans' wide front lawn. The seat and the arch had been made by Joshua's father, who'd been a landscape gardener, and most of the trees and plants in the garden had been nursed by his hands. Andrew was perched on the edge of a rockery facing them, and he was looking fondly at Josh as he spoke, his head inclined in a pose of interest that Saoirse thought couldn't possibly be genuine. Andrew Jackman was very handsome. Saoirse wondered what his life was like in Switzerland, what his wife might look like. Tall and severe, she guessed, coldly beautiful. She imagined herself as the wife of someone like Andrew, wondered whether she'd be able for such a role, hosting dinner parties and cocktail evenings and having opinions on the world and all its workings, knowing things about art and books and music, expressing this knowledge with wit and style, kissing people on each cheek as they arrived and left. She wondered if their mannered speech and gestures would extend to the bedroom, whether they would adopt in their lovemaking the same rarefied, cultured ease and knowingness, whether they'd master each other's bodies as they surely mastered the world they occupied.

She was still thinking about Andrew Jackman and his wife when they reached home, and walked into the kitchen, and found there her mother, being strangled to death.

WILL

Mother's face was purple and her brother's face was white. She was on her back on the floor near the table and one of her shoes was lying near the door and Richard had his hands around her throat and he was making a high, whining sound, a kind of pitched moan, a pulsing *woo, wee, woo, wee, woo, wee*. Mother's hands were raised and she was gripping the sides of his suit jacket. Her legs weren't moving; it was as though that part of her body had shut down already, that she was already half dead. There was a long ladder in her tights and her blouse was riding up over her bra and Saoirse thought, in the kind of muted senseless way that a person will think things in moments of extreme shock, that this looked like a scene from one of the daytime true crime series that Nana loved, like someone had choreographed this whole affair, ripped Mother's tights and pulled her blouse out from the waist of her skirt and up over her breasts, and painted a line of blood from Mother's nostril down as far as her upper lip, and they'd artfully applied a skim of makeup to the skin of Mother's face to make it look such a grotesque colour and so puffed. Any moment now someone would shout, *Cut*, and Richard would stop and Mother would sit up and look crossly at them and tell them to go on away about their business, they'd be finished in a minute, that she'd call them.

She heard then the actual words that Richard was saying. You *will*. You *will*. You *will*. Another impossible thing then: Josh flying through the air. Actually flying. His feet were off the ground and his arms were stretched in front of him and his body was arced in a dive across the kitchen towards Richard's side, and he was on Richard then and Richard was flying too, in Josh's arms, away from Mother, onto the floor at the far end of the kitchen, and they landed on the floor by the stove, and Mother was still, her legs were still and her arms were still and her mouth was open wide in a silent scream and her eyes were rolled back so that her irises had almost disappeared.

Josh now had his knees either side of Richard's neck and his left arm was working up and down and so were Richard's legs and Josh was flying again, in through the archway out of sight, and Richard was standing, and Nana was out of her chair, screaming, Eileen! Eileen! Eileen!

Mother was sitting up now, holding her two hands to her livid throat, her eyes bulging and her lips and chin striated with blood. She was making a gurgling, wheezing sound; she was trying to get up, reaching a hand towards her daughter.

Saoirse moved finally, down to the bloodied floor, and took her precious bleeding mother in her arms.

EVERYTHING

It was just a fight.

That's how we carried on all through our childhoods, Richard and me. If we weren't loving each other we were killing each other. I pushed him off the barn roof one time, you know. Daddy came along and picked him up and told him he was grand. I was above on the roof looking down at him, sure he was dead. He never told on me. But he held me under the water of Dirt Island pond so long a few days later that I breathed in a lungful of water and I saw the light of Heaven before he let me up. He was the smallest of the boys his age but he was always well able for them in a fight because he'd always go that one step further. He put his arm one time right into a hole in the old house wall where we knew there was a nest of rats and he pulled one out and dropped it in our cousin Con's lap. He reached right in through the window of Daddy's car, and Con inside in it wearing his good suit because he was coming with us to a station mass, and plopped a big black rat right onto him. Con soiled himself with the fright. There. Was. Murder.

Mother was smiling while she told these stories, sitting on the couch, a cigarette in one hand from a packet she'd stashed somewhere in her bedroom, and her other hand at her bruised throat, as if to hide the stigmata of her brother's fury. But her smile was brittle and shaky at its edges. She'd never thought that Richard would go so far. He'd walked in unannounced brandishing some kind of a contract that would mean that Mother would be given the worth of the land that her father had left her and he'd be given title to it. But she'd refused to sign and he'd lost his reason, she said. And the worst thing is that I was going to sign the fucking thing eventually. What do I want the hassle of it for? A bit of soggy fucking grass and a dirty pond. I'd have let him have it to fuck if he hadn't been such a fucking *weasel* about it.

Nana wasn't the better of it yet. She'd gotten a terrible fright. Only for young Elmwood, she kept saying. Isn't he a great lad? Only for him. Josh waved away the approbation but Saoirse could see that he was proud of the way he'd acquitted himself, saving Mother and bloodying Richard, then standing nose to nose with him before Richard bolted, leaving his contract behind him in crumpled leaves spread around the kitchen floor, where moments before he'd nearly killed his only sister.

We were always so great with one another, Mother said, from inside her reverie of sadness and regret. He always loved me. And I loved him. Even after everything, I always loved him.

DAYTRIP

Pearl was to spend the day at the farm.

She waited in her pink tracksuit and matching backpack at the bay window, ignoring her favourite Saturday-morning cartoons, wondering aloud where they were, asking of every car that turned into the estate, Is that them now? Is that them? She'd formed an unexpectedly strong affection for Doreen, who'd bounce her on her lap and sing old-fashioned nursery rhymes to her that seemed in their lilting rhythms and nonsensical lyrics to entrance her; she'd open her eyes wide as Doreen sang, jigging Pearl up and down on her lap, and at the end of the rhymes Doreen would open her knees so that Pearl would fall through, then catch her and heave her back onto her lap again, and Pearl would scream in fright and joy. *Ride a cock horse to Banbury Cross, see a fine lady on a white horse, rings on her fingers, bells on her toes, she will have music wherever she GOOOOES!* Pearl was singing the song in anticipation now as she stood watch. And when Chris's car came into view she jumped up and down in excitement, and Nana shook her head and said, What kind of bribery is going on to say that child is gone so fond of the quare one? Anyway, sure what harm? Isn't it grand to think of her above around the land in the fresh air? I love the thought of her little feet set along the paths that my children's feet were set on, and all the children that lived there before them.

So off they went, the odd little family, Pearl strapped into her car seat and Doreen in the backseat beside her, an unnecessary caution, but Saoirse supposed that she was unused to travelling with a child, and that she wanted to maximize her proximity to Pearl now that she had her all to herself for a day. Chris, dear faithful Chris, was shining with happiness at his wife's happiness; he'd brokered this day on her behalf, lobbying Saoirse gently with promises that he wouldn't as much as start an engine while Pearl was within a mile of the machinery, nor would he let her near riverbank, slurry pit, haybarn or road. She'll be glued to Doreen all day, anyway, said Chris. They're thick as thieves these times, thank God.

The hours unrolled pleasantly. Mother took Nana to town and wheeled her to the bakery and then to Gough's where she bought herself a pair of winter boots, declaring that she'd be needing them because she'd be back on her feet by Christmas. Saoirse and Josh spent the day watching films that Josh mocked but then seemed very taken by; the kinds of films that Honey would have dismissed as exploitative trash.

Darkness fell. Mother tried to ring Chris on his mobile but there was no answer. Mother and Saoirse drove to the farmhouse. The door was unlocked, the house was empty and so was the yard.

POOL

The moon was huge and deathly white.

Everything was ghostly in the yard. There was a series of muffled lows from the slatted house and a shuffling and butting as cattle settled against each other for the chill late-autumn night. Why was the house empty? Why was the door left open? Why was Chris not answering his phone? His car was parked between the gable of the house and the haggard wall. The moon was grinning down at them; the moon knew what was going on. Saoirse felt inside her a bitter swell of fear; it was coating the inside of her mouth and clogging up her airways so that she was struggling to breathe; her fingers and toes prickled and a surge of heat coursed through her stomach, countering the weakness she'd felt at the thought of Pearl, lost in the cold night, and it propelled her forward. Where in the fuck are those two fruitcakes with our child? Mother said as she started across the cobbled yard and turned for the path that led through the outhouses to the bottom field.

Saoirse's phone rang. It was Chris. Chris, where are you? We're here in the yard. It's very late for Pearl to be out. Where is she? There was only a low hush of static and wind for second after second, and then Chris's voice, barely audible. I don't know. I don't know where she is. Doreen took her for a walk up the fields hours ago. Up the hill towards Tountinna. She said they were only going as far as the top stile to see could they see shooting stars. There was a thing on the news about them. A meteor shower or something. Saoirse screamed suddenly, JESUS CHRIST, CHRIS, WHERE THE FUCK IS PEARL? WHERE THE FUCK IS MY BABY?

Come on, Mother said, and she took Saoirse by the hand and led her up the path towards the bottom field and they scaled the gate and started uphill, towards the first stile and over it and towards the top stile where they met Chris, washed grey by the moonlight, and they started all three of them up the hillside, and Chris was saying, All it is now is Doreen is after losing track of time and Pearl is well wrapped up, don't worry, don't worry one bit, they'll be up along the path somewhere, I guarantee you, Doreen wouldn't allow any harm to come to Pearl, she . . . she . . . she . . .

Without the full moon's light they'd never have seen her, sitting by the dark pool that opened in the earth where the grass gave way to bracken and scrub and the hill steepened towards its summit, with Pearl sitting in her lap, swathed and hooded in her padded coat, Doreen hunched over Pearl, rocking her backwards and forwards as she slept, and they were perched at the very lip of the black pool that stretched, it was said, down to the centre of the earth.

INFINITY

And now the night drew itself across them.

A high-piled cloud moved across the moon, blotting out all the figures on the hill, Doreen holding sleeping Pearl, Mother and Saoirse standing on the pathway above the pool, knowing through some pulse of instinct not to move towards Doreen who was at its far side, and Chris, standing across from his wife who was whispering, Don't. Don't, Chris. I'm warning you, I'm warning you, don't come near me, don't move another inch. Doreen was on her haunches on the pebbled slope, and Pearl was very still, and all it would take was the tiniest of movements and they'd be in the water. The cloud rolled on and the moon was in the water, smiling up at the small and stricken assembly.

I didn't hurt her, Doreen said. I just gave her something to make her sleep. Bride Cranty used to give it to my mother years ago. I still have a bottle of it. Do you remember Bride Cranty, Eileen? And Mother replied in a shockingly normal voice, Yes, Doreen, I remember Bride Cranty well. Doreen nodded. She was from Travellers, you know, out of Galway. The real old-style Travellers with the wagons and tents that'd come to places like this to fix pots and pans and anything that could be cajoled back to good shape. They put her out, God only knows why. It must have been something terrible. She bewitched oul Jerry Cranty, and he married her. They're the parents then of Mickey Briars that helped you build your new room. Did you know that? I did know that, Doreen. Come on now, we'd better get Pearl home.

Oh, but did you know the real thing about Bride, the thing that she was most known for? Now Saoirse could see that there was no way for Chris to get around the rim of the pool in less time than it would take for Doreen to tip herself and Pearl into the water, and that their only hope was to engage her, to keep her talking, to pretend interest in what she was saying, to pretend to Doreen that they cared about what she was saying, that they cared about her.

She was most known for helping girls and women to kill their babies. That was where you went if you wanted help with your trouble. If you wanted to get your problem sorted out. And this is where she threw the ones that came out whole. Into this pool. It goes down to infinity, you know, this pool does. It's full of little babies and their souls. Oh, Lord, imagine it. All those little lives torn out from their mothers. All the little angels unwanted. I'd have loved any of them. I'd have loved them all.

And Chris, somehow, was beside her. He was lifting Pearl up from her lap. He was holding the child to his chest and Doreen was falling forward, falling, into the cold water.

FOREVER

That's how easy it is to die.

You can tip yourself forward from your heels to the balls of your feet into a spring on the side of a hill and be gone forever. The memory of Doreen's last moments expanded outwards from her centre to fill the world, the universe. Every object and sound and action was informed or inflected or fully composed of the idea of Doreen's death. How she must have felt as the water received her and then closed around her. Did her brain force her body into a struggle, the unconscious animal part of it that wants only to survive, above all else? Did she open her mouth as she sank to draw in water to her lungs? A question that tormented Saoirse most of all was whether her eyes were open or closed as she pitched forward. Saoirse remembered the scene both ways, so one of the memories had to be false, though they both felt real. When she asked Mother if she knew, Mother had gotten cross and told her to stop fixating, to get on with her blessed life, to forget about the whole thing; it's bad enough, Mother said, that they'd been forced to bear witness besides allowing the whole sorry thing to take over their lives.

The pool transfigured itself constantly in her imagination. It was a dark lidless eye, an open mouth, a wet-fanged, gaping maw, a pitch-black portal perfectly round, a jaggedly shaped lake, an inland sea, a puddle. A static and pristine memory was of Chris, looking down at the point where his wife had disappeared, clutching Pearl to his chest. His face in the moonlight had been a sick deathly white and he had said his wife's name in a tone of hushed surprise, as if she'd just given him an unexpected and very thoughtful gift; there was an upward inflection to the first syllable and a dragging of the second, and it seemed in Saoirse's memory almost comical, the suggestion in his voice of loving censure, that he might follow his breathing of her name with *You shouldn't have.*

Everything else was clear in her mind. Her and Mother's progress along the pool's thin stony rim to where Chris stood holding Pearl; taking Pearl from Chris and falling back onto a hock of reedy grass and shaking her gently to wake her; Mother leaning over them both, saying, She's breathing, she's breathing, she's fine, oh, thank you, Jesus, she's alive; and a splash then behind them as Chris entered the water and Mother screaming, No, no, until he surfaced again, and dived again, and surfaced a second time, and a third time, and finally dragged himself out of the eye of Hell and lay drenched and broken beneath the moon.

Doreen was recovered as the dawn broke, from the mouth of a culvert that led possibly to a whole system of underground springs and caves. It was true, then. The pool went on forever.

ABANDONED

Chris said he couldn't live alone.

Not in the house, anyway. She was still there, he said, he could feel her and hear her and sometimes he could even see her, sitting across from him, looking straight at him, asking him why he'd allowed her to die. The house was a nest of ghosts now, his father and his brothers and his wife, flitting in and out of view, and none of them giving him any comfort, but only driving him deeper and deeper into a sense of desperate waste and emptiness. He tried to renew the house, but all of his changes were superficial and easily changed back: furniture rearranged, walls repainted the same colour or repapered in the same dour designs. Nana insisted on being driven up there as often as possible and helped from room to room, as if to re-infuse the house with her presence and her spirit, to overwhelm and exorcize Doreen's dark, lingering residue.

But Chris could find no way to carry on, doing the things he'd always done, before he'd been harassed by death. He called to them regularly now, in the middle of the day, usually just as Mother came home. He talked more than he used to, about remote things, the wars in the Middle East, the American elections. He said one day, suddenly, from his seat at the rail of Nana's bed: This is all your fault, Eileen. If you hadn't turned me down that time, none of this would have happened.

And none of them would have believed him, gentle loving Chris, capable of saying or even thinking such a thing, and neither would he have believed it of himself, until it was said, and couldn't be unsaid. Mother crossed the room to where he sat and bent down to kiss the top of his head, and everything then resumed, as though he hadn't spoken at all.

He sold his sucklers and then his milking cows, and he reduced his small few head of dry stock one by one until the herd was gone. He refused all offers of contract work. He shaved his hair close to his scalp. Jesus Christ, said Nana, when she saw him. God help us, his mind is gone. He rented a small flat in Nenagh from a shyster, a one-bedroom box above a shop on Pearse Street, and he liked it, he said, the noise from the street was company for him, and he was only there at night anyway. He boarded up the windows and the doors of the farmhouse, and when Nana saw this work done she howled in anguish and rose from her chair into the frame of her walker and crossed the dried muck of the yard to the edge of the haggard and she asked Saoirse to take up a handful of soil and to bring it home with her. And when I'm in my grave, she said, you're to throw that down on top of me.

WITNESSING

Life took up its beat again.

Josh made a speech one day about bearing witness. He had no choice, he said. Saoirse wasn't sure what he meant but he was holding both of her hands in his, gripping them tightly, and his brown eyes were fixed on hers, and she knew that he was attempting to evince with his speech an air of profoundness. It's the duty of the novelist to make a record, he said, and she nearly laughed at the studied gravity of his expression. All of these things that happened, all of these dramas, all of these shades of declension between love and its absence, between living and dying, between love and hate . . . It's falling to me to sublimate all of this life into art. It's my *life's mission*.

She couldn't help her laughter then, and he dropped her hands and looked away, and she was sure his lips formed themselves for a moment into a pout. He didn't resume his declarations about bearing witness until a few days later as they drove across the bridge at Ballina in his mother's car and turned towards Scarriff, to see if it was possible to see, through binoculars he'd borrowed from Andrew Jackman, the spot where they'd first made love, from the opposite shore, the Clare side of the lake. Wouldn't it be amazing if we could? And Saoirse had agreed that yes, it would be amazing, but she wasn't sure exactly why. That spot reminded her now of Doreen, watching them from a leafy redoubt by the callaghs path while they made furious love, and the memory burned her a little in her stomach and caused a low fibrillation in her heart.

I just think, he said, as the road climbed into the base of the Clare hills and the lake dropped away on their right side, that I've been put here, in this place, at this time, for a reason. I was drawn back from London, and we had a kind of lovely rhythm for a while, me and you and Honey and my job and her job and our families all sort of humming along in that comfortable dysfunction that seems to be the best any family can hope for, and then Honey left me, and it all seemed bewildering and fucked up, like everything was falling apart, and then it all came together again through you, and it all seemed *ordained*, somehow, directed, like someone had laid a blank sheet before me and commanded me: Write it.

Saoirse didn't reply. She didn't like the suggestion that she was a vessel, empty, passive, a dumb element in some grand divine plan for Josh's life. Nor did she like this talk of Honey and her leaving as a central, defining part of Josh's emotional landscape. She felt diminished, sidelined, duped. The silence between them stretched out along the road before them, into the sweeping bends, and she promised herself that she wouldn't speak, she wouldn't break.

VIEW

It turned out that it was possible.

On the edge of the wooden quay by Woodford pier they sat while Josh trained his sights on the far distant shore. After a few minutes of humming and focusing, sweeping his view slowly across the miles of placid open water, he said, There. There it is. That's our spot. There was a warmth in his voice that pleased her: this was a thing between them that was just theirs; it had no print on it of Honey or any part of their lives before they loved each other. She looked for a long while through the heavy binoculars at the tree, bowed and heavy-limbed, and the particular low branch that formed itself, as though by some intelligent design, into a perfect seat that fitted their forms exactly, and below that kind branch their little beach, flanked by stands of reeds and hidden from the rest of the foreshore by a thick tumult of hedgerow and rush. There was something thrilling about seeing that place from this perspective, from this distance, as though she were looking into the recent past, where their mirrored selves might at any moment appear and lie down on the sand and make love, then sit half clothed and look across the lake, across time, back at themselves.

Please, Saoirse, Josh was saying, and his voice seemed distant, as distant almost as the lake's far shore. Don't think badly of me. I have to tell you something. She knew what he was going to say, and he said it, almost word for word as she'd imagined. I speak to Honey. A couple of times a week at least. I didn't tell you because, well, I don't know really why I didn't tell you. We just talk about things, you know, her film, and the people she was working with, and she's been asked to stay to do the edit, you know? And she says she couldn't pass up the opportunity. And. I don't know.

He didn't know. Neither did Saoirse. What was this thing? She felt, more completely and abjectly than she had in the car, reduced, compressed now to a ball of crumpled nothingness, to a soiled, discardable thing, a fling, a series of seedy assignations on a stony beach and in their childhood bedrooms. She'd been a substitute for Honey, who was in her absence inviolable, superhuman, sanctified, raised up from any possibility of ordinary failing. Josh, she knew in that moment with a desolate conviction, was waiting for his true love to return.

And then things turned again, at least a little. He put his hand around her waist and pulled her close in to his side. She fucked off on us, didn't she? And Saoirse nodded, afraid to speak. And again things turned, almost fully back now to the clean unsullied joy of their early, brimming, thoughtless days, when he said: I love you, Saoirse. I need you. Please. Please, don't ever leave me.

COLLABORATION

At last he came fully to the point.

He wanted her to help him with his book. A new book, not the Billy Shears one. It seemed to him that all of these wild things that happened quietly in this small place needed somehow to be marshalled into art, into something permanent and tangible, something that rendered them into sense. Think of it, he said, and his eyes were so full of happiness and enthusiasm for this new project, his skin so flushed and lustred, that she could feel the heat of it from him, sinking into her.

There's your mother, he said. And that whole weird thing with her brother, and her family disowning her because she got pregnant out of wedlock, and even when they got married your dad not being good enough for them, and your mother then being this warrior woman raising a baby on her own and keeping herself intact in spite of all the odds being stacked against her, and fighting for every inch of ground she makes, and that witty way your nana and your mother speak, and Paudie and the IRA stuff, and Chris and Doreen, and you, and the whole thing with the way Pearl came to be, and how she has this mad famous father who doesn't know she exists and whom she doesn't know about. It's just, it's just, *begging*, you know, to be made into a proper story. It's like, everything that happened to me up to this point happened to me so that I'd be here, now, to tell this story.

This seemed a very self-centred way of looking at life. Saoirse struggled in her memory for a name, of the boy who drowned in a pool while gazing at his own reflection, believing himself to be the centre of all things. She remembered Sister Laelia's face as she'd told them the story. Oh, yes, mad about himself he was, girls. Like many men, you will find as you go through your lives, he was *enraptured* by himself. Narcissus! That was it. And Doreen suddenly appeared at the centre of her vision, toppling silently forward, her emptied hands at her side, crouched almost double, her body jerking as her knees momentarily dug into the earth and took her weight, and the soles of her flat brown shoes flashed in the moonlight for a split second before the water closed blackly over her.

But Josh's straining ambition also ignited in her a warm fantasy. She imagined them at a wide desk, side by side, beneath a high corniced ceiling, holding pages in their hands. Pearl, teenage, pretty and casually fashionable, addressing Josh as *Dad*. Mother and Nana safely ensconced in their own wing of the wide, airy apartment they all lived in. Chris and some new wife and their golden-haired child living in an apartment downriver, with a view of spires and domes from their window, of a sparkling world, ancient and new and filled with love.

CHAPTERS

So they agreed then how they'd go about the whole thing. In the mornings while she sat with Nana and Pearl she'd make notes. That's how he put it: sat. I don't just sit around, she said, I'm a *caregiver*. I provide care for my grandmother as well as caring for my child. She was proud of the fact that, between them, she and Mother had made sure that Nana had never gotten a bedsore, not even when she'd been almost fully immobile in the heavy weeks and months when she first came home from hospital after her stroke. And also that Nana had not seemed to deteriorate: she'd kept her weight steady, and her spirit, and she'd done her exercises, and she'd taken all her medicines as prescribed, and they'd babied her, Saoirse knew, but Nana was not averse to being babied, and she had slowly and surely rallied back to something of her old self, a facsimile, but strong and clear.

So that was telling him. Oh. Okay. Well, I mean, is there any time in the mornings that you might be able to make a few notes? Any quiet time when maybe Nana is napping, or Pearl, or both of them? Or maybe when one of Nana's shows is on, *Murder, She Wrote* or *Highway to Heaven*? My idea is that we do this thing day by day, where I collect your notes in the evening and write a chapter that night based on what you've given me, and I want you to give me everything, everything, don't hold back, pretend it'll never be read by anyone but me, and I mean, chances are that it won't. It's nearly impossible to get anywhere as a writer, the only true measure of success is to have something actually written, something that exists.

Saoirse was excited by the idea. It felt like something that would link them inextricably forever, that would form itself from their separate parts into a whole that comprised them both. She liked the idea of allowing Josh to see inside of her, but at a remove, so that the stifling embarrassment of revelation would be absent; she wouldn't have to feel herself redden as she whispered some truth about herself or feel his discomfort, feel him struggling to respond, to know how to reply, or to act on her words. This could be a way for them to allow each other direct and unfettered access to their true beings. She would say things, and he would respond to those things, interpret her truths, transmute them into something beautiful, something worthwhile and good. She was going to let him know her in a way that he couldn't know Honey, and in doing so she would graft her soul to his so that they'd be one entity, and all others would necessarily be forsaken.

These thoughts filled only a moment, and as they dissipated she felt a stab of unexpected shame, and she began to write.

ZONES

Mother heard it in the bookie's.

Actually, she was told directly. The man who came in to tell her wasn't even himself a betting man. The strip of land that Mother had been left, from the roadside edge of her father's farm to the pond and the island of clay that gave the whole townland its nickname, was part of a massive re-zoning of farmland for development. Years of lobbying had been done, many palms had been greased, and it was about to be announced. That was why Richard had been so murderous about getting it off her. Her share was going to be the most valuable part of the whole farm. The fucking rat. The sneaky little rat bastard. Anyway. What about it? She laughed and pulled on her fag and sat at the dining table half turned towards the window. Daddy will be laughing down at us. He'll have done all this designedly. Why couldn't he have left me out of it?

So there was that. Something that would have to be dealt with. Mother's idea was to do nothing. To leave the land fallow, to refuse to sell, not to give an inch. But then there was something else. Another day at the bookie's, another revelation, this time from a woman who worked in a solicitor's office and was an old school friend of Mother's. She'd done the paperwork, arranged the maps and the ancient deeds and all the conveyancing, and she was only saying this now because it was a dirty stroke that was after being pulled, and if it was ever found out that she'd spoken to Mother about this she'd be fired, but she couldn't not, she said. The way it was being done was all so underhand. She knew enough about the law and how people could manipulate it to know that Chris was being badly used, was having a fool made of him, that his judgement was clouded by grief. It might not be too late, she told Mother, to look for an injunction while a case was prepared to claim that Chris couldn't properly have been party to a contract because he wasn't of sound mind when he agreed to the deal.

Chris had sold the farm. The whole fucking thing. Every blade of grass. Without even an advert or an auction to get the best price, without knowing, it seemed, that the farm was part of the re-zoning business, that it was going to be worth a hundred times more than it was as farmland. Or maybe he didn't care. Either way, he'd done it all himself, off his own bat. Nana wasn't to be told. Nana was never to find out, Mother told Saoirse. She'd been so happy when she'd signed the land over to Chris, and relieved, believing it to be in safe hands.

And who had bought the farm? Who the fuck do you think? Who else would have bought it? Richard, of course. Sweet Richard.

ACID

It didn't suit Mother, having secrets from Nana.

After all their years together, living in one another's pockets. It was a miracle how they loved each other still. They knew what was said about them. Wasn't it the queerest set-up you ever heard of? A widow and her dead husband's mother, and they together now ten times longer than the couple had been, and they solid wrapped in one another. They understood each other, you see. They had a way of being around one another that was based on each having a natural grasp of the other's particularities and peccadilloes; they nursed one another's wounds without ever seeming to do so, they fed one another's spirits, and an outsider looking in, listening to the seeming rancour of their discourse, hearing the names the younger woman would call the older woman, the way she'd threaten almost daily to strangle her, to suffocate her, to drown her, to shoot her, to take her to the fucking vet, could not be blamed for supposing them to be mortal enemies, and for worrying that the older woman's welfare was in danger, that her very life was under constant threat.

That was how it was with Mother and Nana. That's the kind of admiring talk you could hear at a meeting of the local chapter of the Irish Countrywomen's Association, or at a sale of work or in the yard of the church. You could hear less admiring talk too, of course, about their joint stewardship of their small household, how the child in their custody had turned out to be a right little strap, a bold little floozy, and how the child she herself had borne, and no one knowing who the father was but there was no shortage of suspects, was heading the same way, being overly indulged, paraded around the roads by her mother, who was being well paid by the state for her life of indolent luxury, by the taxes of decent people, and that Gladney boy and his long hair dragging along behind them. Or Elmwood. Whatever he was. What was he at all? Not the man his father was, anyway, God rest him.

Mother knew what people said. Fuck them all. Talk never bothered Mother, but truth was important to her. And she could keep Nana from hearing the truth for a while, but she couldn't bear to have a lie between them, and so she sat one evening at the rail of Nana's bed and she took Nana's hand in hers and she told her what Chris had done, and Nana said nothing in reply except that Chris was to be brought to her, and when he drove in from his flat in town he stood at the end of Nana's bed with his hands hanging, and she said nothing to him, she just sat back against her pillows and looked at him and cried silently, and her tears scored him, like acid on his bare flesh.

EXCHANGES

So all that work was done in secret and in silence.

But everyone knew. All over the country it was the same. Stories flew everywhere, told wryly for the most part, or with an undertone of admiration, or sometimes with disgust. In a half-language of conjecture and innuendo, reputations were blackened, everyone presumed guilty with no chance of proving their innocence, or any need to do so, in fairness. People were made wealthy, it was said, who'd never known wealth before. Mother heard stories of men wrapping bundles of banknotes in cellophane and hiding them all over the countryside. Burying wads at the ends of gardens, stashing waterproofed thousands in holes dug in the loamy soil at the edges of bogs; lucre buried in forestry and foreshore, in common land but far from common paths. And in exchange for those remittances great swathes of God's green earth were differently coloured now on giant maps that were posted on the walls of council offices everywhere. Sole traders incorporated themselves into companies to limit their liabilities. Workers were coaxed from abroad with promises of years of work and high wages. There'd be roads and schools and houses and hotels and fountains where before there'd been only grass and trees and soft mucky soil, useless organic growth fit for nothing but the chop.

And Richard rolled one weekday evening up the narrow boreen, briars from the hedges reaching across almost to their opposite numbers, and he surveyed the land he'd tricked from his sister's brother-in-law, that he'd bought through a proxy before the new zones were official or announced, and he began laying out lines around the farm and house, Nana's house, where her marital bed still stood on its four stout legs, where her good crockery was still ranged along the shelves of the ancient dresser in the parlour, where the walls and floors and ceilings still vibrated with the ghostly frequencies of generations of Aylwards, by blood or by marriage, all of them in their way still present.

So Mother said, Fuck this. And she drove the main road west towards her childhood home and up a boreen just as narrow but better cultivated, and she walked the jagged route of the bounds of her bequest, holding before her a folio map that she'd been given by her father's solicitor on which was marked in red the outline of what she owned. As Richard processed at his leisure up the bottom field and skirted over towards the neighbours' houses to be sure to be seen, so did Mother stand out on the road along Dirt Island in her wellingtons and yellow jacket and her film-star sunglasses, her long hair tied back jauntily and a white summer flower cocked from her hairband, and she flamboyantly saluted her neighbours old and new who were walking there, so that they knew, so that Richard would know, so that no one would be in any doubt, that she was the Queen of Dirt Island.

HEART

Through all the new dramas Saoirse made her notes.

Josh brought her home a jotter from Limerick with a brown cover, soft and fragrant like expensive leather, but he said that it was moleskin. She started that night to fill it with her memories of all the things that had happened to her, that she'd seen happen around her, that she'd heard said. From the very first things she could clearly remember, the white-shirted man in the garden with the old-fashioned camera that he looked down into, his reflection in the window glass, bent to his task, tall and black-haired, who, as she'd discovered, was Richard, so his and Mother's big falling-out must have come years after she'd said it did, to the time she'd heard Mother and Nana talking about how her name might sound to Americans, to the time the baby blackbird had broken its little body against the front window and died in the garden; she poured onto the notebook's thirsty pages a plot in tidy slanted words of her life and her family's life, and she found things in her memory that she hadn't been fully aware of, things that had lain unexamined and unfelt inside of her for all these years.

The images in her head, of Oisín and his kind, jigging father, and Oonagh Jones's narrow red face, and Breedie Flynn's deep abstract fund of sorrow, and the fuzzed, amorphous night of Pearl's conception, formed themselves into words that clicked pleasingly together into sentences, and she remembered Sister Laelia's words as she handed her back her essay book in English class in second year, words she'd paid no heed to at the time: You have a real talent for telling stories, Miss Aylward. It'll serve you well if you honour it. She was so consumed some days by the task that Nana had to call her four or five times before she looked up, or Pearl had to put her hand right onto her arm and shake her from her trance, her burgeoning visions.

But it wasn't up to her to tell the stories. Her job was to hand Josh the notebook every evening when he called after walking up from the main road, with more pages filled with her impressions of the past and of her family's past, and to take it back from him every morning when he called on his way back down to get the bus to work, and she missed him in the evenings now, and Nana and Pearl missed him too, and even Mother asked now and again, Is Josh not going to stay a while? Are ye not going out tonight? But she was happy with this temporary sacrifice and with the way her memories bloomed one from the other through the weeks, and she imagined sometimes Josh on a stage, holding an award, his hand extended towards her, his love, his muse, and herself, radiant, smiling back at him, her two hands on her heart.

SWEET

It was almost funny the way it happened.

In Limerick one Saturday, as they shopped from a list in Roches' Stores compiled by Kit Gladney, who was tired, she said, of her ancient, chipped crockery, her time-stained utensils, they met a girl who worked with Josh in the factory. Small and peroxided, with lines of silver studs along the outer edges of her ears, a single stud on the side of her nose and one through the tip of her tongue so that her words were slightly lisped, she greeted Josh almost violently, raising her hands to him and pushing against his chest, smiling and saying his name with playful shock, adding *y* to the end of it, drawing out her appended syllable like he was a child in a pushchair: Josh-*y*, what are you doing in from the boondocks on a Saturday?

Josh reddened so deeply and so suddenly that Saoirse was afraid for a second that there might actually be something wrong with him. He made a choking sound. The girl was ignoring her; she was standing in a vaguely combative pose, her runnered feet wide apart. There were fake rips all down the legs of her jeans and she was wearing an AC/DC T-shirt. The band were grinning demonically at Josh from the girl's heavy chest, and Josh was looking wild-eyed at the girl, and the girl was making a bemusedly quizzical face at him, and no one was looking at Saoirse but she was studying the scene closely, and some formless truth floated towards her and stopped, like a dream sitting just beyond the reach of memory.

Claire, he said at last. Hi. How are you? It's nice to see you. Is it? the girl said, and she laughed, thin and high. I'm sorry now, Joshy, but I can't say the same. I fucking hate being reminded of work on a Saturday. You country bumpkins shouldn't be allowed in from the farms at the weekend. Do you not have crops to milk or cows to harvest or something? And Josh laughed nervously along with the girl, and still he hadn't made any move to introduce Saoirse to her; nor had he looked in her direction. The wash of blood was receding from his face but the tops of his cheeks and his ears were still bright red, and Saoirse felt herself grimly fascinated by the physiology of his panic.

The girl swung her shining face towards Saoirse and smiled, wide and insincere, and there was a small livid swell around her tongue stud, and her teeth were small and sharp, and she said, Oh, at last. The mystery woman. Well, it's great to meet you. I feel like I know you! The way this lad tucks his phone between his shoulder and his ear to talk to you at work, it's so CUTE! His little whispers he thinks we can't hear! It's sickly fucking sweet. Oh, well. I suppose you are called *Honey* after all!

EASY

But I told you I spoke to Honey.

    You didn't fucking tell me you were telling her you loved her. Saoirse was sitting close against the passenger door so that the gap between them was as wide as possible. Josh's driving was erratic: he changed lanes in the middle of a roundabout and an angry horn sounded behind them. FUCK OFF, Josh shouted, and for a second Saoirse thought he was shouting at her. It's not like *love* love, it's just ordinary *friendship* love, it's just the word, really, you know the kind of person Honey is, the kinds of people she hangs around with and works with, that's how they communicate, that's the way they speak, it's all love this and love that and I love you and you love me and it's all bullshit.

    Bullshit it's all bullshit. *You*'re bullshit, Josh. You've been making a fool of me. Just don't talk to me. I don't want to know. Just get me fucking home and then you can fuck off, fuck off, fuck off.

    She didn't want to know. The range of possible truths to the situation formed itself into an oddly comforting cushion of uncertainty around her. He might be telling the truth about the casualness and hollowness of his professions of love. It might be true that he had to speak to her during work because she was still in some remote place and only in range of a phone mast for a small morning window every few days. Maybe they were properly broken up and he'd told Honey he loved Saoirse now, that he was sorry, that they were sorry.

Maybe they laughed together about her. Maybe he read bits of her notes to Honey and they laughed at her stupid stories, her stupid accidental life, her daughter's dismal conception, her foul-mouthed mother and her bewildered grandmother and the comedies and tragedies of her uncles and of Doreen and all the foulness and sweetness and sorrows and mysteries of her tiny world, and why in the fuck anyway would he want to write her story, or base a story on her memories? Why hadn't she asked herself what he really wanted from her? Why had she debased herself so completely, with such idiotic joy?

She heard clearly in her imagination, as if she were in the car with them, leaning forward from her seat so that their faces were almost touching, Honey's voice, in a high pitch of anger, saying, Serves you right, you stupid, faithless little bitch, serves you right for trying to steal my man, for thinking you could have him, for stabbing me in the back, you and your stupid heart, trying to give it to someone who didn't want it, he only used you, he used you, and I told him to do it, I told him you'd look after him, and you did, you stupid little girl, you gave him what he wanted, what all men want. An easy fuck.

LIBERTIES

B ut Saoirse didn't really think that Honey would ever say
that, even if she knew.

She got out of the car and slammed the door and Josh
waited for a minute before he drove away. Nana asked her what
was wrong. Nothing, she said, and Nana tutted. Come here
and sit beside me, she said. Look, lovey. You have to mind your
heart. I'm sorry now I ever encouraged you with that boy. I was
too gung-ho altogether about the whole thing. And Saoirse
turned to her grandmother, who'd buried two of her three
sons, and she saw in her face nothing but love, and concern for
her, and her grandmother was squeezing her hand, saying,
Take life easy, my darling. You only get one, and you have to
do your best to be happy. When Josh texted later that evening
and asked if she'd go away with him the next weekend, she
thought again of her grandmother's gentle exhortations before
replying, Yes.

On a Saturday night in a hotel bar near the Salthill prom-
enade on Galway city's western edge, after a day spent walking
hand in hand through Spanish Arch and along by the quays to
Eyre Square and back down to Spanish Arch again through
the unhurried throngs on Shop Street, stopping here and there
to listen to buskers and to eat and to browse in shops, after
Josh bought her a Claddagh ring in a little jeweller's on a

corner near Melia Bridge and put it on her finger with an air of tender reverence, and kissed her fingers and told her that he loved her, really loved her, and she'd felt as happy as she could ever remember feeling, everything, in a moment, was ruined.

A man in a rugby shirt, on the edge of a group of noisy men in rugby shirts, with English accents and high, excited voices, put out his hand as she passed on the way back from the toilets and slapped her arse, a short, stinging slap, and when she turned around he smiled and winked and said, Sorry, love, but that arse was *asking* to be smacked, and his friends' whoops and cheers rang against the walls and echoed back against themselves, and the bar was a distorted chamber of feedback and wide-open mouths and eyes for a few beats of her heart, and Josh then was standing by her, with his hand tight on her arm, and he was leading her away, back to their booth.

There were too many of them. It was just a little slap. It happens all the time. The guy was drunk. These things she allowed Josh, and she allowed herself to forgive him. But she saw when she looked at him, every time she looked at him from then on, a different Josh, who was looking down at his swollen knuckles with pride, even as Honey, his love, his woman, screamed that he was stupid, stupid, stupid to have fought for her.

LACERATIONS

The truth of it all lay unvoiced between them, festering.

That his passion for her, if it existed at all, was of a different nature. She couldn't put words on her thoughts that didn't sound petulant or immature. You punched a guy for her but not for me. You let those fucking jock bastards laugh at me. If it was Honey's precious arse that got smacked, if it was Honey, if she was, if you were, if, if, if, if. I'm the one, you're the one, she's the one.

Josh drove in silence along the winding roads back inland from the bright city, through towns and villages where people sat in happy groups outside pubs and on tree-lined greens, as a thick cloud of resentment and disappointment filled the air between them, clogging her airways so that she found herself struggling to fill her lungs. There was a thick blockage in her throat, a throbbing pain across her chest. She wound down her window so she could breathe the wind.

As though it had unexpectedly struck him that it might act as a kind of mitigant, as the basis of a new accord between them, or a bloody sop across their mutual lacerations, Josh suddenly said, in a voice that was almost shockingly loud and upbeat: Our story! He reached across for her hand, and she let him take it, but only briefly. It's nearly finished. I want you to read it. I really think you'll like it. I don't know what I'd have done without you, Saoirse. And it struck her then that he'd never really told her anything about why he seemed so badly to need her notes; he'd said something vague about how they'd anchor his art to life, allow him to strike for some pure truth. She wondered at her own lack of fear, how she'd so willingly committed her life to paper for him, laid her heart before him, allowed him the run of her past. And again she allowed a terrible vision to assail her, before forcing it away, of Josh reading her notes to Honey, saying, Wait, just wait until you hear this bit, and of Honey laughing, saying, Oh, babe, oh, babe, what a stupid girl.

But she didn't care now. She wanted just to crawl into her bed and cuddle Pearl into her and have her mother come in and kiss them both goodnight and listen sleepily to her mother's voice and her grandmother's voice in the near distance as they mingled together, warm and kind and familiar, Mother telling Nana the news of the day, and Nana exclaiming here and there and asking, who? Who? And Mother saying, You know, the one, the big one with the cod eye and the smelly husband, and Nana laughing her wicked laugh, and everything could be reset to how it was before, the time before these burning feelings she couldn't put a name on that afflicted her, that wouldn't leave her be.

MANUSCRIPT

It was typed on Kit Gladney's ancient typewriter that she'd used for her bookkeeping.

He'd tied it with a band of navy cloth, bowed at the front, like a gift, and placed it in a padded envelope. He'd handed it to her with a slightly embarrassed air and a gleam of something in his eyes, something that seemed to demand of her an answer, or a reassuring gesture, some word or action to indicate that this transaction would rebalance the deficits between them of love and trust. He'd walked away then, and she'd watched him until he turned the corner onto the main road and out of sight, and he seemed so slight, so vulnerable, so small and alone beneath the vault of sky and the ancient trees that lined the road that she'd felt a sudden wash of tenderness, an impulse to run after him and to press herself against him and tell him that everything was going to be okay, that it didn't matter about the rugby players or about Honey or about whatever he'd written. All that mattered was . . . But she didn't know what she'd say then. She didn't know herself what mattered for him or between them, and she felt oppressed by her lack of knowledge, the burden of all the world's uncertainties.

When she opened the bow and removed the band she saw that the top page had typed across it THE QUEEN OF DIRT ISLAND, and below that title the words, A Novel, and below that, By Joshua Elmwood. She couldn't see herself on the pages at first. The person the story was about seemed older, to be looking back from middle age on a life lived. It was a few pages, almost the whole of the first chapter, before she realized that the character was something like Mother, a woman widowed early in her marriage and left to raise her child alone, and as the child grew older page by page she saw hints of herself, saw lines of her own story contorted, distorted, extended, pulled apart and refashioned into short paragraphs and bursts of dialogue, but everywhere that Josh had taken from her a seed the thing that grew from the seed was unrecognizable, alien, monstrous.

She stopped reading and sat for a while beside Nana, whose left arm had recovered some of its strength and her fingers some of their dexterity, so that she was able, slowly, with stubborn determination, to knit again. The soft clack of her needles and the low hum of the song she was singing to herself and the murmurs of Pearl from the dreamworld she occupied as she read on the couch were the sounds of safety, of warmth, of pure uncomplicated existence, of simple love.

She looked across the room at the manuscript sitting on the window-ledge. She knew now how foolish she'd been. To have looked into Josh's sad eyes and seen herself reflected there, to have fallen, and nearly to have drowned.

DISTORTIONS

There was Mother in the yard telling a teenage boy to go home and wash the grass off of himself.

But *grass* now had another meaning: the distorted Mother of the manuscript was some kind of leader, and she was accusing the boy of being untrustworthy, of being related to someone who'd betrayed Mother or some kind of shadowy group to which she belonged. The boy was a foot soldier and her lover; he was desperately in love with her and she toyed with him, manipulating and tormenting him, and ultimately discarding him. Go home, she said, and wash the *grass* off of yourself, and from Josh's twisted Mother the words were hissed and spat and contained a threat of violence or of death.

There was a man who had the shape and voice of Paudie, pleading with the Mother-woman whose name in Josh's manuscript was Sadie, holding up to her his bloodied hands and his broken fingers, saying, I swear, I swear, I never told the Tans a thing, they done that to me and I never told them a thing, and the woman saying, You'd better fucking not have, you'd better fucking not have, before striking him so hard across his face that he falls to the floor and lies crying there while the woman stands above him, telling him he'll be getting no more warnings, that if he fucks up again she'll send him straight to Hell. And she does, a few chapters later: he goes to prison and is found strangled in his cell, murdered on the Mother-woman's orders.

On the neatly typed pages of Josh's manuscript, with here and there notes in biro written in his backwards-slanted hand between the double-spaced lines, or words crossed out with corrections written over them, was a girl, the woman's daughter, and the woman loved her dearly but the girl was sad, and spent a lot of her time looking at pictures on the walls of the father she never knew, and her mother, the titular queen, would tell the girl that her father was a hero, that he'd died a hero's death in the name of freedom, but the exact nature of his death was not revealed until after the halfway point, near the hundredth page, when the man sailed to England and drove a car that was stuffed with explosives into the centre of a city, and the explosives detonated prematurely, killing him, killing a dozen bystanders, so that the operation, planned and directed by his wife, was only partially successful, and cost the organization its bravest, most faithful lieutenant.

And there before her eyes, in black ink on white paper, with no corrections or handwritten notes, was a girl being abandoned by her best friend, and carried by a group of men into a van, and the van door sliding closed, and the girl the next day beneath a tree, bruised and torn, silent as death.

And the words ran like blood along the page.

PARALYSIS

In the light-filled room at the back of Kit Gladney's cottage, Joshua Elmwood wept.

It felt strange to see him actually cry, this boy who seemed forever on the edge of tears. She'd suspected, in the more fraught moments of their relationship, his constant air of sadness to be an affectation, an instrument of manipulation: how could she argue with him when he was so burdened? He used his delicate sorrows as a battering ram, smashing his way into people's hearts, where he could reside until he was bored, taking what he wanted. It felt at times as if he filled the space around his selfhood with a padding of grief and vaguely intimated sorrows, so as to move without resistance towards what he wanted. And what he'd really wanted from her, she had thought, in her most abject moments, was the comfort of her body, the knowledge of her willingness to offer herself to him. He gorged himself on love.

Now, it seemed, she had subjugated him. She had thrust his manuscript at him when he opened the door, and he had stood bewildered, shirtless, looking down at the floor at their feet where it lay, unenveloped but back in its bow, and back up at her, and down again at his months of work, making wild plots from the images she'd offered of her mother and her uncles and the father she'd never known, ignoring the truths she'd offered about her life and about the things of which she was composed, transforming the workings of her family's hearts into an outlandish plot, making monsters of them.

Now in his room he was trying to explain. The house was otherwise empty so he could shout if he wanted, but he didn't, not at the beginning of their pitiful exchange at least: he was lobbying her, canvassing her good opinion, trying desperately to bring her around to his vision for what he had written. He was holding the bowed pages level before him and out from his body towards her like a votive offering, as if she were a priest who would take it from him and lift it into the sight of God, and sanctify it, gain for it divine gratitude. She was surprised at her own ineloquence, her inability to express clearly the things she'd had it in her mind to say, all the way up from the estate and through the village to the entrance from the main road to the narrow lane that ran through the Jackmans' green hillside fields, over the stile at the halfway point by the closed gate and through Kit's blooming garden. She'd formed a small barrage of censure in her mind, and had each point poised for deployment, and now she found herself overheated and tongue-tied in the face of his desperation, hobbled by her pity for him, her insistent, clawing shame at herself for causing him this pain, and she found herself paralysed within a corona of ferocious love.

EXPLOSIONS

But her paralysis broke when he said it wasn't enough.

What she'd written wasn't enough? No, no, hold on, that's not what I meant, I meant that I couldn't use *just* what you'd written about for the story, I had to add on bits for dramatic effect, to make a proper story out of it, something that was exciting, that would give a reader a sense of something beyond the mundane, something that would lift the characters from the page into their imagination, into their hearts.

Tears were streaming freely now, shockingly, down his cheeks and onto his bare chest, and he looked thin and pale and younger than his years, like a boy in need of a father's hand on his shoulder, or a mother's arms around him, like a boy in need of a hug, in need of reassurance, of unconditional love. It occurred to her that the best thing that she could do would be to take the manuscript back from his shaking hands, and to lead him across the wooden floor to the bed, and sit with him there, and take him in her arms and hold his head against her chest and run her fingers gently through his hair and soothe him, shush him like a baby, kiss his cheek and his ear and his forehead, tell him he was brilliant, that she knew nothing, that his book was amazing, that she was only joking about it being a fucking insult, a horrible bastardization of her experience and of her family's struggles, and of her mother's nature.

But instead she watched from outside of herself as she stepped towards him and stopped, and shouted, FUCK YOU, JOSH, FUCK OFF WITH YOUR FUCKING SNEER-ING BULLSHIT BOOK, YOU THINK YOU KNOW ME, YOU KNOW NOTHING ABOUT ME, I'M SORRY I EVER WENT NEAR YOU, I'M SORRY I EVER GAVE YOU A WORD OF MY LIFE, I'M SORRY I EVER LET YOU TOUCH ME, YOU MADE A FOOL OF ME, I KNOW WHAT I MEAN TO YOU, NOTHING! AND YOU'RE NOT A WRITER, YOU JUST THINK YOU ARE, YOU'RE A LITTLE BOY WHO SULKS TO GET HIS OWN WAY AND USES PEOPLE AND NO WON-DER HONEY FUCKED OFF, SHE COULDN'T STAND YOU ANY MORE!

And he dropped the manuscript then and a small cloud of dust rose around it and billowed minutely outwards into the rectangle of light that spilt from the long window in the room's south-facing end wall. And Saoirse lunged forward to pick it up, but he pushed her back and bent himself to pluck it from the floor and she was falling backwards, shocked to silence at his push, and the manuscript was in the air between them now, and its bow was broken, and its pages were swirling about each other in a miserable desultory cloud, and Joshua Elm-wood was pivoting about on the balls of his bare feet and he was punching the wall, and screaming, Fuck, fuck, fuck, fuck, fuck.

FLAMES

And then the world came back to them.

There was a thud at the door. Then Kit Gladney's voice, Joshua! What the blazes is going on? Who's in there with you? Joshua stood in the centre of his scattered pages, wearing only a pair of beltless, dirty jeans, his head inclined towards her, his brown eyes bright with rage and tears, his shoulders heaving up and down, his fists still clenched, blooms of bright blood on his skinned knuckles. Then Moll's voice, What is it, Mam? Is he all right? And the soft sound of the two women retreating back along the short hallway to their kitchen, where their open fire perpetually burned, a steaming pot hung always on an ancient crane across it, and Saoirse could just make out Kit saying, They're having a row, let them have their privacy, don't you know how youngsters are? Everything that goes wrong is the end of the world for about five minutes and then it's all grand again.

Joshua was kneeling on the floor of his bedroom and Saoirse noticed from where she sat on the edge of the bed a canvas that was fixed to the easel by the window. There were two figures painted on it in heavy swirls of oil, lightly abstracted, overlong of limbs and face but beautiful in their surreal way, a dark-skinned female figure with long hair rendered in heavy black dots and flecked here and there with bright colours like flowers, and a lighter-coloured male figure with long brown hair and dark eyes, and both figures were naked, facing each other, their aspects angular and feline, like images she'd seen in Sister Patricia's history class of figures on the wall of an Egyptian tomb. Gods.

Saoirse didn't feel in that moment as though there was any truth in Kit Gladney's words. It wouldn't all be grand again. Nothing would ever be grand again now that the truth of things was lying scattered on the floor between them. That her story wasn't enough for him, that she wasn't enough for him, that the inhuman figure in his story was preferable to him as a subject than her mother, her brave, glorious, beautiful mother; that the faithless, weak-willed girl in his story was somehow his truth of who and what she was; that the long-limbed goddess on the canvas in the stream of windowlight was his true love, and not her, not her.

She watched as silently he gathered to himself his jumbled sheaf and made it a tidy rectangle again, tears dropping from him all the while and forming themselves into wet islands on the wood, an archipelago in reverse, and she was about to speak, to tell him this, how his tears looked, but he was walking towards the door, and he was in the kitchen, and she could hear his mother and his grandmother exclaiming as he committed his manuscript, every single page of it, to the flames of their eternal fire.

ASHES

So all that work was done and then undone.

She thought at first that he must have a copy, that his burning of the book had been a show, a ritual, a kind of threat. She walked embarrassedly out to the kitchen and towards the hearth where he stood, past his mother and his grandmother, who offered kindnesses from her store of garnered wisdoms. Ye'll have this all forgotten before the sun is set. A lot worse will happen ye before ye're twice married! Is that the thing you were writing all these months now, burnt inside in the fire? Well, there's no unburning it now, so you may as well go into your room and put on a shirt or a gansey and take that girl down to the village or into town and treat her besides acting like the Rapture is here and you haven't your sins confessed. Go on away and dress yourself in the name of all that's decent, will you, besides going around like a fecking madman burning things. Go on now, Josh. And Kit turned to Saoirse as her grandson slunk away, heaving from himself a shaky sigh as he went that felt and sounded like a sigh that contained a good share of relief. Saoirse, love, I don't know at all what went on between ye, and I'm in no position to judge anyone, or to mediate between two people, but I know you since the day you were born, the same as I know that boy his whole life, just about, and there's neither of ye grown up fully yet, and may

God spare ye from growing up another while. Enjoy yourselves, lovey. Don't take life so seriously. Whatever will be will be.

Saoirse had a sudden mad vision of Kit and Moll bursting into song, *Que sera, sera,* and she smiled at the thought, and the two women smiled back at her, and Moll patted the empty chair beside her, and Saoirse sat, and Kit poured a cup of tea for her and stirred a spoon of sugar into it without asking if she wanted it, but she did want it: she wanted the warmth and sweetness of this strong tea and these women's company, and for Josh to stay in his bedroom a while longer until the smell of burning paper was gone from the room and all the blue smoke of his immolated passions was wisped into the wide chimneyway and back to nothingness.

At last he emerged, fully dressed and washed-out, and he held her hand as they walked downhill in silence. His hand was warm in hers and he squeezed her fingers gently in a slow, pulsing rhythm as they walked, as though his blood were coursing with such force that his veins were widening and contracting with his heartbeat. He kissed her at the edge of the road, softly on the lips, and he turned and started back uphill, and that was their parting done.

REVERSALS

Everything went to shit for Richard.

Mother felt sorry for him. The man who'd ejected her from her mother's funeral, who'd come to her house and tried to strangle her, who'd gloried in her estrangement from her family for the better part of a lifetime, had run down his devil's luck. Some big cheese made a speech about *indiscriminate and excessive re-zoning of land* and about local authorities *acting against planning advice.* There were rumblings and mumblings about possible reversals and investments were put on hold. The pleadings of vested interests, the besuited speechmaker said, should not have been factors in local councillors' decisions to re-zone land for development. A man was shot dead on a farm out past the Ashdown Road, a boy really, whom Saoirse remembered from school being ignored or picked on, and nearly always on his own. He'd been left the farm by his parents and he'd refused to sell it to a consortium of developers and the pressure he'd been put under had crushed his reason, it seemed, and he'd pointed a shotgun at police and they'd killed him.

Nana's farm was coloured back to green on the council's map. Richard had bought a pig in a poke. Mother shook her head in pity. Poor Richard, she said. All he ever wanted was to be like Daddy, but he couldn't, so he tried his best to be the big I-am. And now the only part of Daddy's farm that was really valuable to him is in my name, and the land he thought he'd stolen from us is worth what it was always worth: what you'll get from it in fallow grants or creamery cheques, and neither of those amounts to very much.

Mother thought to cash in her inheritance quickly. You need to do something with your life, she told Saoirse. You need to get some kind of qualification. What was I thinking all this time letting you moon around after that fucking hippie Joshua Elmwood and you not having a piece of paper to your name to say you were anything or could do anything? If I sell Dirt Island we can send you into the city to get a trade, hairdressing or something, and we'll be able to set you up in business. Saoirse said she didn't want to be a hairdresser but Mother got a bit wicked then and she threw the lipstick she'd been smearing on herself across the sitting room. You'll be whatever I fucking say you'll be, missy! But everyone, Pearl and Nana and Saoirse and whoever of the neighbours overheard Mother's bellowed exclamations, knew that she was all sound and fury.

On a rainy Sunday afternoon Mother drove herself to Richard's box of a fake Georgian house on the lip of the shallow valley that lies between the Arra Mountains and the Silvermines, and she sat with a puffed-out, red-eyed Richard and his sweet-faced docile wife, and she proposed to them a deal, and they accepted.

REVERSIONS

So Richard got Dirt Island back and Chris got back the farm.

When Nana heard the news she was silent for a while. Then she nodded slowly and she reached out her hand towards her daughter-in-law. Thank you, Eileen. There wasn't much more to be said. Chris was summoned from his bolthole in Nenagh and told that he was to begin to restock, and that the farmhouse was to be opened up, whether or not it was lived in. He accepted these edicts with silent grace and set about the work of revivifying his crumb of the earth.

Nana declared that the miracle that had been worked had extended itself outwards and enveloped her in its magic. She began to spend the best part of her days out of bed, and to move herself slowly around, out to the garden even, just to stand in the frame of her walker in the sunlight, or under the rain. Who would ever have thought she'd enjoy the rain so much? She who had always lived in fear of being caught out with no umbrell. It's umbrell-*a*, Mary, Mother said. It's not, Nana replied. I never in my long life heard that word spoke like that except by you, Eileen Aylward. Umb*rell* it is, and always was. Maybe ye big fancy-pants farmers out abroad in Dirt Island calls it that but I never once in my life heard it said that way and I'll die my death before I ever say it that way. Umb*rell*, umb*rell*, umb*rell*.

Suit yourself, you fucking oul bitch, Mother said. I don't care what you call it. Let everyone laugh at you above at mass and you going around the vestibule like a madwoman looking for your *umbrell*. It's all the one to me. If it's all the one to you why are you still talking about it? Mother then mumbled something about smothering the old hag the first chance she got and Nana sat primly upright on a kitchen chair, regarding Mother through sparkling eyes, and declared herself to be as happy as a woman could be who was a widow and who'd seen two children to their graves. And Mother sobbed suddenly, shockingly, standing in the middle of the kitchen floor, and Pearl looked up from her drawing at the kitchen table, and Nana's eyes widened, and Saoirse stood from her seat by the stove and went to move towards Mother who put up her hand to keep her, to keep all of them, at bay, separate from her, outside of the realm of her emotion.

And after a moment they all returned to their previous aspects. Mother wiped away the tear that had escaped onto her cheek. She started a story about a man who'd come into the bookie's with no shirt on, just his big ignorant hairy belly sticking out in front of him, and how she'd refused to take his bet until he dressed himself. Proper order, said Nana. That's my girl.

KNOWLEDGE

A letter from Honey.

In blue ink on yellow paper she had written in her loop-
ing, forward-slanting hand a letter seven pages long. Saoirse
held the sweetly perfumed leaves out from herself. She couldn't
look directly at them for a while. She sat on her bed and Pearl
sat before her on the floor, asking, What is it, Mam? What
does it say?

I miss you and I love you all. That was the first thing it
said. The force of her relief caused Saoirse to cry out softly,
Thank God. For what? Pearl asked. For nothing, love. I'm just
happy to have a letter from Honey. And Josh? Yes, and Josh.
Hmm, Pearl said, and she shook her head and settled back to
her stewardship of her Lego village. Now, Miss Doctor, you
have to go to work. In the hostipal. There's been an accident,
oh, no.

Saoirse's heart calmed and she was able to lay the pages on
her bed in sequence left to right. She knelt then before them as
in prayer, and it occurred to her that she'd never knelt and said
a prayer outside of mass, not once in her life. She felt a strange
thrill at this tiny transgression, at the thought of a celestial
arbiter who might judge her to be mocking the Faithful with
this mimicking of the aspect of worship, and she smiled at the
idea. But still she couldn't read past the opening lines that said,

Dear Saoirse, I miss you and I love you all. What could be in the next seven pages? What did Honey know?

Everything. She knew everything. Josh, it seemed, had made a full confession. She was but a chalice for his sin, and their time together now was compressed into this mortifying explication. Honey wrote with a cold hand of all the precious and painful things that comprised what she called their *love affair*: the tiny half-moon of shingle beach where they'd first fallen together to the ground at the edge of the lake, the long afternoons they'd spent in the cottage in Knockagowny, how the months had progressed and the world had fallen away; she knew about the English guys in Galway, how Saoirse had felt let down, how she'd reacted to Josh's parlaying of her story into a series of vulgar dramas, how they'd parted. She heard herself whispering in her mother's voice, in her grandmother's words, He spilt his fucking guts. Good Jesus, he spilt his fucking guts.

But there was no blame in Honey's words. She just wanted Saoirse to know that she knew everything. And Saoirse knew that in Honey's mind the fullness of her knowledge preserved somehow the inviolability of the love between her and Josh. In its absence of censure and its unrelenting, oppressive openness, it was as cruel as Honey was able to be. And deepest was the sting of its closing lines. I'll always be Pearl's godmother. I'll always be your friend. Love, Honey.

SINGERS

Pearl was thirteen before she asked about her father.
It had never seemed to occur to her that she was missing something, that her family was composed differently from most of her friends' families. Years later she would tell Saoirse that she'd presumed that the smiling man in the framed photos on the mantelpiece and the sitting-room wall whom her mother and her grandmother and her great-grandmother all referred to unthinkingly as Daddy was her daddy, too. She'd never asked about him because she'd had no questions; she'd absorbed so much of his ambient spirit that he felt part of her, and she felt herself part of him, until one day, the day that she finally asked, it had struck her that the man in the photos was her grandfather, and that someone else must be her father.

Saoirse told her child her father's name. What? Like the singer? He *is* the singer. The singer is your father. Saoirse told her daughter word for word the truth. Pearl sat on the couch with her hands in her lap, her long legs stretched before her. She looked for a moment as though she might cry. Wow, she said eventually, and she rose and crossed the small room to where her mother stood in front of the fireplace. Wow, Mam. So he has no idea that I exist? And Saoirse shook her head. How is that possible? And Saoirse had no answer, nothing prepared to say to her daughter beyond the bland plot points of the truth. She felt a bilious acid wave of panic rise from her stomach into her throat. But Pearl smiled at her. So that's where I got my voice!

Pearl was a popular girl, kind-hearted, trusting and confident, and she told her friends the story she'd been told. Only a few of them disbelieved her and a handful laughed at her and talked behind her back, carrying home to their parents the story of who Pearl Aylward thought she was, and she knew then who her real friends were, as far as anyone can know such a thing.

She resolved that she would someday meet this man and tell him who she was, and she tucked her resolution away in a private, safe place, where she could draw it out sometimes and consider it, and plan it, and visualize it, how it might play out, how he might look at her, what he might say. She uploaded all of his songs to her iPod and she listened to podcasts of him being interviewed, and he mentioned once or twice that he'd love someday to be a father.

She rewound his recorded voice and replayed him saying this, and some part of her that harboured a natural, inborn wisdom, an intuition about the vast world outside her tiny world, and the people she'd someday find there, knew that, no matter how she felt or how much unanswered love she stored, things would play out as they would.

HIKERS

Chris found himself involved with a woman again.

Nana took it much better this time. For all her pretence at disapproval and all the digs she and Mother bandied between them about the ebullient young American he'd hooked up with, she was relieved for him. It wasn't right, the way he'd been living, between the farm and the flat in town that he seemed so determined to cling on to, even though he had a lovely job done on the farmhouse, and it a solid fright to God to think of it sitting empty and resplendent after all the generations of Aylwards that had filled it, but at least it was better than the way Nana's own people's house had gone, just a few stones now rising up from a ditch and no trace of any of the people who'd lived their lives and died their deaths there, but wasn't that the way of things? We're all being broken down piece by piece back towards the earth from where we rose.

Anyway, whatever about that. Wasn't it the luck of God the way it happened? That people started to ask if they could hike up through the yard and across the pasture towards the hills and up into Tountinna. And Chris, of course, wasn't able to say no. Once they kept to the path, he said, and didn't leave any litter behind them, they were welcome to pass through. Nana told him he was making a rod for his own back with his easy acceptance of gangs of foreigners from Dublin and God knew where else tramping in about the place looking out of their mouths. And Chris, for all his big talk telling people not to leave litter, took to picking up the bottles and papers and sandwich crusts and apple cores himself that people inevitably dropped along the trail, and one day he was asked about the house by a young woman with a Yankee accent who was walking on her own: she wanted to know if she could have a look inside; then she asked if she could rent it, or rent a room in it at least, and whatever else happened Nana didn't know and nor did she want to know but nature will take its course between people, and nature took its course.

There they are now above, and the house being used as a *writers' retreat*, I ask you, what are they retreating from?, and the old slatted house and barn turned into apartments, rented out all summer long and most of the winter, and Chris and the one with the blonde hair and the big bust and the loud voice living above in one of the apartments as man and wife and didn't she land on her feet? Texas, she's from. Didn't she come a long way to dig her claws into a fine little farm and a finer man? Anyway, we'll say nothing. Look what happened last time. God bless them.

HOME

Time will wind its own sweet way.

We have no choice but to keep up. Our bodies know they're getting old but sometimes our hearts have to be reminded. Nana declared that her *knockouts* were reminders. Shut up, will you? Mother said, but Nana would persist. Another knock*out*, loves, she'd say from her hospital bed, or from her own bed after being brought home. I won't suffer many more before the big day comes. And when it does you'll have to be very good to Eileen. She'll be in an awful way after me. She hardly ever lets on a thing, of course, but I know. We're living in one another's pockets now the bones of forty years. It'll be a big change for her. She could go downhill, you know, without me to give her a gee up. Mother said that was bullshit. She couldn't wait to get her house back. Fucking oul bitch had the whole place taken over.

Not long after Pearl's fourteenth birthday, on a Friday afternoon as spring stretched into summer and the cherry blossom was in full glorious bloom, Nana asked to be taken for a drive. So they set off together, first to the Gladneys' cottage, where they found Moll and Kit Gladney, who was more than a century old and still possessed of all her faculties, and Ellen Jackman, sitting on an old bench beneath the flowering apple trees, and Nana sat in her wheelchair with them for a while and they talked easily about nothing much, before saying goodbye, goodbye, old friends, we'll see ye, please God, and may it stay fine. Moll Gladney walked down with them to the halfway stile and she bent at the gate and kissed Nana's cheek.

Over then they went to the far side of the Jackman ranch and up Nana's own boreen to the house she'd married into when war had still echoed from the Continent, and flour couldn't be got, nor fuel, for love nor money. Chris wasn't there and the house was locked. A few scrawny wayfarers lolled around the outside of the converted barns. Nana tutted at the sight of them and asked Mother to turn around, to drive over by the old water pump at Pallas, then down to the lake. And all the while inside the car the four women talked and laughed, none of them mentioning the truth they all knew well, and Nana remembered stories she hadn't thought of for a long time, and they sat all four of them at the end of the short pier in Youghal Quay, and Nana told them about the time her husband had driven a motorbike clean across the lake to Clare and it one big sheet of ice. Lord, he was a foolish man at times.

Home they went. Nana said she'd had a lovely day. She smiled at them as one by one they kissed her goodnight. She was holding Mother's hand as she closed her eyes.

QUESTIONS

Do not turn over your papers until I say so.

The woman's voice was high and screechy. It vibrated in Pearl's ears. For a desperate moment she worried that all the things she'd memorized would be scrambled into an insensible paste of words and images. She lowered her head and breathed in deeply and held the air inside herself and exhaled slowly, just as Honey had said to do in her email. Hold your nerve, my love, and try to do your best, and what will be will be. She looked at the people around her in the hall, their comforting, familiar shapes, bathed in shafts of dusty light from the high windows. Some of them had been her friends and classmates for the last thirteen years, since her very first day in Youghalarra National School, when her mother and grandmother and great-grandmother had walked her to the classroom door and Mammy had cried a bit and Granny had told her to cop on and Nana then had told Granny to cop on herself and they'd nearly started one of their fights right there in front of all the other children and parents and the teacher, and they'd all hugged and kissed her in turn, and she'd loved that first day, making giraffes from pipe cleaners and learning a song about a bird building a nest, and sitting on a grown-up seat and watching the pretty teacher draw cartoon cats and dogs on the blackboard.

And now it all boiled down to this. A series of questions on the far side of this thin blue sheet. And another series tomorrow and the day after about other things, and by the end of next week it'd be all over and she might or might not get enough points to go to Mary Immaculate College to train to be a teacher herself, and if she did, she did, and if she didn't, well, she'd think about that when it happened. Or didn't happen.

Turn your papers over! The woman's voice rang against the distant back wall and the gym's high ceiling, feeding back on itself so it sounded like three voices. She really ought to lower her pitch a little bit. It wasn't fair on people who already had frayed nerves to jangle them further with such a shrill sound. And there was something wrong with the exam paper. The words on it were moving about and blurry as though they were under water. Blocks of words were swimming away one from the other and spreading out past the paper onto the desk.

She put a hand to her throat and caressed the miraculous medal her great-grandmother had given her just before she died. Nana had rubbed it against the glass of a case that contained the relics of Saint Thérèse of Lisieux, the Little Flower of Jesus. Pearl didn't believe in any of that stuff. But still she gripped her medal tight and closed her eyes against her rising panic.

ANSWERS

She thought about the day the books arrived.

Nana watching through the window as the postman reversed slowly in the driveway. Here he's on. Look at the head of him. He goes around cock of the walk spouting shite like he's the feckin' postmaster general. Do ye remember the time he was there at the door petting Pudge from next door and going on about how dogs loved him, how they were always following him around? And I said to him, That's because you don't wipe your arse properly!

Mary! Shut up, will you! He'll hear you! Nana then telling Granny that she didn't care a damn if he did or not, he was only half a man anyway, his townie arse cocked inside in a grand van and there was never a postman in this parish since Paddy Gladney, God rest the good man, and he pedalling up hill and down dale day in day out in every weather with his bag of letters and his basket filled with packages, and that was before he started his day's work for the Jackmans. Lord, Paddy was a proper man, not like this article. How close to the fecking door does he want to get? He'll be inside in the kitchen in a minute!

Her mother then at the back door and the postman offering to lift the box in for her, and her mother saying it was okay, and the postman saying, Lift with your legs, not your back.

Nana's voice then floating out from her perch by the living-room window, He's some feckin' know-it-all, wouldn't you think he'd lift it himself if he's such an expert, and the jolly postman smiling, winking, calling back from his cargo doors, Hello, Mrs Aylward! and Nana shouting back, Oh, hello, Francis, love, is it yourself? Tell your mother I was asking for her!

And her mother then, her hand shaking a little as she cut the tape along the top of the box, and drawing from it a book with a picture on its cover of a woman in soft silhouette standing on a narrow sandy shore in the shadow of a drooping tree, and rays of sunlight bursting through the tree's long fronds and sparkling on the water at the woman's feet, and Nana leaning on her walking frame in the archway, squinting, saying, Isn't it a funny name for a book all the same? and Granny saying, Will you shut up, you oul bitch! And the four of them sitting in quiet wonder and happiness at the kitchen table with the advance copies of the book heaped in its centre, the book that had caused a three-way bidding war, making headlines before anyone had read a word of it.

And now, half of a decade later, Pearl Aylward's eyes focus, and she reads the first question in her English exam: *Discuss, with reference to the text, the representations of womanhood in Saoirse Aylward's novel* The Queen of Dirt Island.

BEGINNING

Pearl was beautiful, inside and out.

On a morning in May, with barely a cloud in the sky, and a gentle breeze carrying the rich scent of new growth down from the hillsides and sunlight dancing inside among the boughs and bursting flowers of the cherry blossom, sending pink-white dapples across the concrete of the driveway and up the clean walls of their little house, Saoirse Aylward helped her daughter to load her bags into the boot of her car. Eileen Aylward said she'd drive. You will in your arse, her daughter said. We'll never get there if you drive. She'll miss her flight. Eileen hadn't the heart for the fight and she went to sit in the back seat, but her granddaughter protested, saying, No, Granny, please sit in front, or it'll just feel weird. Oh, for God's sake, what does it matter who sits where? Eileen Aylward, who had regained some articles of her faith with Nana's passing and her advancing years, was shaking Lourdes water over her granddaughter, and over the roof of the car, and onto the ground around them, and when the bottle was nearly empty she took from her handbag a small flat vial of oil with which she anointed the child, the woman, who had just finished her exams at Mary Immaculate College where she was studying to be a teacher, and had deferred her second year so that she could go wandering about the wide, dangerous world, and her grandmother prayed to God that this impulse wouldn't last too long, that she'd miss them so badly that she'd take one quick look at what was out there and turn immediately for home, and that she'd stay here, safe inside their small house, swathed and cosseted in love.

Eileen Aylward looked at her daughter, who was wearing dark glasses in an attempt to hide the sight of her eyes, puffed and red-raw from crying, and something swelled inside her chest, a smothering upsurge of love and pride and searing worry, about these women, these people who held her heart in their hands, for whose happiness she'd give her life, and she sat in beside her daughter and she turned to her granddaughter and told her to put on her seatbelt, and she asked her again did she have all of her things, her purse and her cards and her emergency cash and Nana's miraculous Little Flower medal, and Saoirse said, Don't forget, love, Josh and Honey will be waiting to collect you at JFK, and if you don't see them straight away you're not to set a foot beyond Arrivals, and Pearl said, Yes, Mammy, I know.

And they pulled out onto the road and down to the main road and they turned for the town and the motorway, and Pearl Aylward felt her world at once contracting and expanding, and she felt her heartbeat steady in her chest, as they moved, those women, through the green country, into the blue horizon.

ACKNOWLEDGEMENTS

Love and thanks:

To you, Reader, for giving me reason to continue down this winding road; to the people who toil in the book trade, for keeping us writers afloat in these stormy seas; to my friend and editor, Brian Langan, for helping me so patiently and expertly across the line, yet again; to Kirsty Dunseath and Fiona Murphy, who loved these Aylward women from the start; to Kate Samano for her diligent stewardship of this text; to Larry Finlay and Bill Scott-Kerr, whose faith is unwavering; to Fíodhna Ní Ghríofa, Patsy Irwin, Alice Youell, Lilly Cox, Hazel Orme, Catriona Hillerton, Jenna Brown, Keltie Mechalski, Patrick Nolan, Annika Karody, Sorcha Judge, Sophie Dwyer, David Devaney, Alison Barrow, and everyone at Doubleday, Transworld, Penguin Random House Ireland, and Penguin US for all of your support and your incredible work; to the whole PRH rights team for championing my books around the world; to all of my translators and international publishers for retelling my stories around the world with such passion and grace; to Kennys of Galway for their incredible support and friendship; to Owen Gent and Marianne Issa El-Khoury for clothing this book so beautifully; to Joseph O'Connor, Sarah Moore-Fitzgerald, Eoin Devereux, Emily Cullen, Kit de Waal, and all of my dear friends, colleagues and students at the

University of Limerick, my sanctuary and my second home; to my uncle Brendan Ryan, my loved and trusted early reader; to my sister Mary, my archivist, publicist, marketer, strategist and most ardent supporter; to my mother, Anne Ryan, who hates being mentioned, but who is the ground beneath us and the sky above us; to my dear John, Lindsey, Aoibhinn, Finn, Christopher, Daniel and Katie; to Betty Sheehan, Ethel Hartnett, the Ryans of Ballyrusheen, the Shearys of the world, the Cremins of Woodhaven, and all of my extended family and in-laws; to Thomas and Lucy, who fill my darkest days with light; and to Anne Marie, who holds my hand and my heart, and to whom I owe every single word.

And:

In memory of Charlie Sheehan, our gentle hero.